WIT
NEW

....

...

....

....

......

.....·

.....·

....

....

....

Pleas·
   sho

THE LARKVILLE LEGACY

A secret letter…two families changed for ever.

Welcome to the small town of Larkville, Texas, where the Calhoun family has been ranching for generations.

Meanwhile, in New York, the Patterson family rules America's highest echelons of society.

Both families are totally unprepared for the news that they are linked by a shocking secret. For hidden on the Calhoun ranch is a letter that's been lying unopened and unread—until now!

Meet the two families in all 8 books of this brand-new series:

THE COWBOY COMES HOME
by Patricia Thayer

SLOW DANCE WITH THE SHERIFF
by Nikki Logan

TAMING THE BROODING CATTLEMAN
by Marion Lennox

THE RANCHER'S UNEXPECTED FAMILY
by Myrna Mackenzie

HIS LARKVILLE CINDERELLA
by Melissa McClone

THE SECRET THAT CHANGED EVERYTHING
by Lucy Gordon

THE SOLDIER'S SWEETHEART
by Soraya Lane

THE BILLIONAIRE'S BABY SOS
by Susan Meier

'Now, let me inside the house, show me where I can eat and sleep, and get out of my life.'

She'd meant to stay icy. She'd meant to stay dignified. So much for intentions.

Her last words were almost hysterical—a yell into the silence. No matter. Who cared what he thought? She flicked the trunk lever and stalked round to fetch her suitcase. Her foot hit a rain-filled pothole, she tripped and lurched—and the arrogant toe-rag caught her and held her.

It was like being held in a vice. His hands held her with no room for argument. She was steadied, held still, propelled out of the puddle and set back.

His hands held her arms a moment longer, making sure she was stable.

She looked up, straight into his face.

She saw power, strength and anger. But more.

She saw pure, raw beauty.

It was as much as she could do not to gasp.

Lean, harsh, aquiline. Heathcliff, she thought, and Mr Darcy, and every smouldering cattleman she'd ever lusted after in the movies all rolled into one. The strength of him. The sheer, raw sexiness.

He released her and she thought maybe she should lean against the car for a bit.

It was just as well this place was a total disaster; this job was a total disaster. Staying anywhere near this guy would do her head in.

TAMING THE BROODING CATTLEMAN

BY
MARION LENNOX

All the characters in this book have no existence outside the imagination of the author, and have no relation whatsoever to anyone bearing the same name or names. They are not even distantly inspired by any individual known or unknown to the author, and all the incidents are pure invention.

All Rights Reserved including the right of reproduction in whole or in part in any form. This edition is published by arrangement with Harlequin Enterprises II BV/S.à.r.l. The text of this publication or any part thereof may not be reproduced or transmitted in any form or by any means, electronic or mechanical, including photocopying, recording, storage in an information retrieval system, or otherwise, without the written permission of the publisher.

® and TM are trademarks owned and used by the trademark owner and/or its licensee. Trademarks marked with ® are registered with the United Kingdom Patent Office and/or the Office for Harmonisation in the Internal Market and in other countries.

First published in Great Britain 2012
by Mills & Boon, an imprint of Harlequin (UK) Limited.
Harlequin (UK) Limited, Eton House, 18-24 Paradise Road,
Richmond, Surrey TW9 1SR

© Harlequin Books S.A. 2012

Special thanks and acknowledgement are given to Marion Lennox for her contribution to THE LARKVILLE LEGACY series.

ISBN: 978 0 263 22811 3

Harlequin (UK) policy is to use papers that are natural, renewable and recyclable products and made from wood grown in sustainable forests. The logging and manufacturing process conform to the legal environmental regulations of the country of origin.

Printed and bound in Great Britain
by CPI Antony Rowe, Chippenham, Wiltshire

Marion Lennox is a country girl, born on an Australian dairy farm. She moved on—mostly because the cows just weren't interested in her stories! Married to a 'very special doctor', Marion writes for the Mills & Boon® Medical Romance™ and Mills & Boon® Cherish™. (She used a different name for each category for a while—readers looking for her past romance titles should search for author Trisha David, as well). She's now had more than seventy-five romance novels accepted for publication.

In her non-writing life Marion cares for kids, cats, dogs, chooks and goldfish. She travels, she fights her rampant garden (she's losing) and her house dust (she's lost). Having spun in circles for the first part of her life, she's now stepped back from her 'other' career, which was teaching statistics at her local university. Finally she's reprioritised her life, figured what's important and discovered the joys of deep baths, romance and chocolate.

Preferably all at the same time!

Newcastle Libraries & Information Service	
C4 686259 00 D6	
Askews & Holts	Oct-2012
ROMANCE	£13.50

PROLOGUE

HE'D failed.

Jack Connor stood at his sister's graveside and accepted how badly he'd broken his promise to his mother.

'Take care of your sister.'

He'd been eight years old when his mother walked away. Sophie had been six.

What followed was a bleak, hard childhood, cramming schoolwork into his grandfather's demands for farm labour, and caring for his sister in the times between. Finally he'd escaped his grandfather's tyranny to the luxury of wages. From there he'd built a company from nothing. He'd had no choice. He'd been desperate for funds to provide the professional care Sophie so desperately needed.

It hadn't worked. Even though he'd made money, the care had come too late. For all that time he'd watched his sister self-destruct.

Sophie's social worker had come to the funeral. Nice of her. Her presence meant there'd been a whole three people in attendance. She'd looked into his grim face and she'd tried to ease his pain.

'This was not your fault, Jack. Your mother wounded your sister when she walked out, but the ultimate responsibility was Sophie's.'

But he stared down at the grave and knew she was

wrong. Sophie was dead and the ultimate responsibility was Jack's. He hadn't been enough.

What now?

Return to Sydney, to his IT company, to riches that had bought him nothing?

He stared down at the rain-soaked roses he'd laid on his sister's grave, and a memory wafted back. Sophie at his grandfather's farm, on one of the occasions his grandfather had been so blind drunk they weren't afraid of him. Sophie in what was left of his grandmother's rose garden. Sophie pressing roses into storybooks. *'We'll keep them for ever.'*

Suddenly he found himself thinking of horses he hadn't seen for years. His grandfather's horses, his friends from childhood. They'd asked for nothing but food, shelter and exercise. When he'd been with the horses, he'd almost been happy.

The farm was his now. His grandfather had died a year ago, but the demands of Sophie's increased illness meant he hadn't had time to go there. He guessed it'd be run-down. Even the brief legal contact he'd made had him sensing the manager his grandfather had employed was less than honest, but the bloodlines of his grandfather's stockhorses should still be intact. Remnants of the farm's awesome reputation remained.

Could he bring it back to its former glory?

Decision time.

He stared down at the rain-washed grave, his thoughts bleak as death.

If he was his grandfather, he thought, he'd hit something. Someone.

He wasn't his grandfather.

But he didn't want to return to Sydney, to a staff who treated him as he treated them, with remote courtesy.

The company would keep going without him.

He stood and he stared at his sister's grave for a long, long time.

What?

He could go back to the farm, he thought. He still knew about horses.

Did he know enough?

Did it matter? Maybe not.

Decision made.

Maybe he'd make a go of it. Maybe he wouldn't, but he'd do it alone and he wouldn't care.

Sophie was dead and he never had to care again.

CHAPTER ONE

ALEX Patterson was having doubts. Serious doubts.

On paper the journey had sounded okay. Manhattan to L.A. L.A. to Sydney. Sydney to Albury. Albury to Werarra.

Yeah, well, maybe it hadn't sounded okay, but she'd read it fast and she hadn't thought about it. A few hours before she'd reached Sydney she was tired. Now, after three hours driving through pelting rain, she was just plain wrecked. She wanted a long, hot bath, a long, deep sleep and nothing more.

Surely Jack Connor wouldn't expect her to start work until Monday, she thought. And where was this place?

The child she'd seen on the road a way back had told her it was just around the bend. The boy had looked scrawny, underfed, neglected, and she'd looked at him and her doubts had magnified. She'd expected a wealthy neighbourhood—horse studs making serious money. The child looked destitute.

Werarra Stud must be better. Surely it was. Its stock-horses were known throughout the world. The website showed a long, gracious homestead in the lush heart of Australia's Snowy Mountains. She'd imagined huge bedrooms, gracious furnishings, a job her friends would envy.

'Werarra.' She saw the sign. She turned into the driveway—and she hit the brakes.

Uh-oh.

That was pretty much all she was capable of thinking. Uh-oh, uh-oh, uh-oh.

The website showed an historic photograph of a fabulous homestead built early last century. It might have been fabulous then, but it wasn't fabulous now.

No one had painted it for years. No one had fixed the roof, mended sagging veranda posts, done anything but board up windows as they broke.

It looked totally, absolutely derelict.

The cottage the child had come from had looked bad. This looked worse.

There was a light on somewhere round the back. A black SUV was parked to the side. There was no other sign of life.

It was pouring. She was so tired she wasn't seeing straight. It was thirty miles back to the nearest town and she wasn't all that sure Wombat Siding was big enough to provide a hotel.

She stared at the house in horror, and then she let her head droop onto the steering wheel.

She would not weep.

A thump on her driver's side window made her jump almost into the middle of next week.

Oh, my…

She needed to get a grip. Now.

You can cope with this, Alex Patterson, she told herself. You've told everyone back home you're tough, so prove it. You're not the spoilt baby everyone treats you as.

But this was…this was…

Another thump. She raised her head and looked out.

The figure outside the car was looming over the car window like a great black spectre. Rain-soaked and vast, it was blocking her entire door.

She squeaked. Maybe she even gibbered.

Then the figure moved back a bit from the car window, letting light in, and she came back to earth.

A man. A great, warrior-size guy. He was wearing a huge, black, waterproof coat, and vast boots.

The guy's face was dark, his thick black hair slicked to his forehead in the rain. He had weather-worn skin, stubble so thick it was close to a beard, and dark, brooding eyes spaced wide and deep.

He was waiting for her to open the car door.

If she opened it, she'd get wet.

If she opened it, she'd have to face what was outside.

He opened it for her, with a force that made her gasp. The rain lashed in and she cringed.

'You're lost?' The guy's voice was deep and growly, but not unfriendly. 'You need directions?'

If only she was, she thought. If only…

'Mr. Connor?' she managed, trying not to stutter. 'Jack Connor?'

'Yes?' There was sudden incredulity in his voice, as if he didn't believe what he was hearing.

'I'm Alex Patterson,' she told him. 'Your new vet.'

There were silences and silences in Alex's life. The silences as her mother disapproved—as she inevitably did—of what Alex was wearing, what she was doing. The silences after her father and brother's fights. Family conflicts meant Alex had been brought up with silences. It didn't mean she was used to them.

She'd come all the way to Australia to escape some of those silences, yet here she was, facing the daddy of them all.

This was like the silence between lightning and thunder—one look at this man's face and she knew the thunder was on its way.

When finally he spoke, though, his voice was icy calm. 'Alexander Patterson.'

'Yes.' Don't sound defensive, she thought. What was this guy's problem?

'Alex Patterson, son of Cedric Patterson, Cedric, the guy who went to school with my grandfather.'

She put a silence of her own in here.

Son of…

Okay, she saw the problem.

She'd trusted her father.

She thought of her mother's words. *'Alex, your father is ill. You need to double-check everything....'*

'Dad's okay. You're dramatising. There's nothing wrong with him.' She'd yelled it back at her mother, but even as she'd yelled it, she knew she was denying what was real. Alzheimer's was a vast, black hole, sucking her dad right in.

She hadn't wanted to believe it. She still didn't.

She'd trusted her father.

And anyway, what was the big deal? Man, woman, whatever. She was here as a vet. 'You thought I was male?' she managed, and watched the face before her grow even darker.

'I was told you were a guy. His son.'

'That's my dad for you,' she said, striving for lightness. 'A son is what he hoped for, but you'd think after twenty-five years he could figure the difference.' Deep breath. 'Do you think you could, I don't know, invite me in or something? I hate to mention it when the fact that I'm female seems to be such an issue, but an even bigger deal is that it's raining, I'm not wearing waterproofs and it's wet.'

'You can't stay here.'

This was bad, she thought, and it was getting worse.

But her dad's fault or not, this was a situation she had to face, and she might as well face it now.

'Well, maybe you should have told me that before I left New York,' she snapped, and she hauled herself out of the car. She was already wet. She might as well be soaked, and her temper, volatile at the best of times, was heading for the stratosphere. 'Maybe now I don't have a choice.'

Deep breath, she thought. Say it like it is.

'I,' she said, in tones that matched his for iciness and more, 'am at the end of a very long rope that stretches all the way back to New York. It's taken me three days to get here, give or take a day that seems to have disappeared in the process. I applied for a job here in good faith. I sent every piece of documentation you demanded. I accepted a work visa for six months on the strength of a job with a horse stud that looks—' she glanced witheringly at the house '—to be non-existent. And now you have the nerve to tell me you don't want me. I don't want you either, but I seem to be stuck with you, with this dump, with this place, at least until the rain stops and I've eaten and I've slept for twenty-four hours. Then, believe me, you won't see me for dust. Or mud. Now let me inside the house, show me where I can eat and sleep, and get out of my life.'

She'd meant to stay icy. She'd meant to stay dignified. So much for intentions.

Her last words were almost hysterical—a yell into the silence. No matter. Who cared what he thought? She flicked the trunk lever and stalked round to fetch her suitcase. Her foot hit a rain-filled pothole, she tripped and lurched—and the arrogant toerag caught her and held her.

It was like being held in a vice. His hands held her with no room for argument. She was steadied, held still, propelled out of the puddle and set back.

His hands held her arms a moment longer, making sure she was stable.

She looked up, straight into his face.

She saw power, strength and anger. But more.

She saw pure, raw beauty.

It was as much as she could do not to gasp.

Lean, harsh, aquiline. Heathcliff, she thought, and Mr Darcy, and every smouldering cattleman she'd ever lusted after in the movies, all rolled into one. The strength of him. The sheer, raw sexiness.

He released her and she thought maybe she should lean against the car for a bit.

It was just as well this place was a total disaster; this job was a total disaster. Staying anywhere near this guy would do her head in.

Her head was already done in. She was close to swaying.

Focus on your anger, she told herself. And practicalities. Get your gear out of the car. He's going to think you're a real New York princess if you expect him to do it for you.

But he was already doing it, grabbing her cute, pink suitcase (gift from her mother), glancing at it with loathing, slamming the trunk closed and turning to march toward the house.

'Park the car when it stops raining,' he snapped over his shoulder. 'It'll be fine where it is for the night.'

She was supposed to follow him? Into the Addams Family nightmare?

A flash of lightning lit the sky and she thought it needed only that.

Thunder boomed after it.

Jack had reached the rickety steps and was striding up to the veranda without looking back.

He had her suitcase.

She whimpered. There was no help for it, she whimpered.

Her family thought she was a helpless baby. If they could see her now, they'd be proven right. That's exactly how she felt. She wanted, more than anything, to be back in Manhattan, lying in her gorgeous peach bedroom, with Maria about to bring her hot chocolate.

Where was her maid when she needed her most? Half a world away.

More lightning. Oh, my…

Jack was disappearing round the side of the veranda. Her suitcase was disappearing with him.

She had no choice. She took a deep breath and scuttled after him.

He showed her to the bedroom and left her to it. Headed to his makeshift study and hauled open his computer. Grabbed the original letter.

Could he sack a worker just because she was female?

Surely he could if she'd taken the job under false pretences, he thought, reading the first letter he'd received.

My son, Alexander, is looking for experience on an Australian horse stud. Alex is a qualified veterinarian and is also willing to take on general farm work. The level of pay would not be a problem; what Alex mostly wants is experience.

My son.

He flicked through the emails, printing them out. After Cedric's first letter he'd corresponded directly with Alex. *Her.* There was no mention of what sex she was in her emails, he conceded. They'd been polite, businesslike, and they hadn't referred to her sex at all.

Yes, I understand the living conditions may be rougher than I'm accustomed to, but I'd appreciate even a tough job. My aim is to work on horse studs in the States, but getting that first job after vet school is difficult. If I do a decent job for you, it may well give me the edge over other graduates.

He'd expected a fresh-faced kid straight out of vet school, possibly not understanding just how tough it was out here, but ready to make a few sacrifices in order to get the job. Despite the conditions, Werarra produced horses with an international reputation. This would be a good career step.

He'd never have employed a woman.

He hadn't wanted to employ anyone, but sense had decreed he had no choice. This place had deteriorated to the point of being a ruin. The horses took all his attention. The house was derelict and the manager's cottage even more so. Brian, the guy who'd managed the place for his grandfather, preferred to live a half a mile down the road on the second of the farm's holdings. Jack had expected him to keep on working, but the moment Jack arrived he'd lit out, abandoning his wife and kids, disappearing without trace.

The letter from Cedric Patterson, addressed to Jack Connor, had come when he was overwhelmed. Despite his misgivings he'd thought, a vet…plus someone who could help with the heavy manual work like getting the fences back in order… The manager's house was unlivable, but maybe a kid could cope with sharing the big house with him.

He'd written back to Cedric explaining that the Jack he was writing to, the Jack he'd gone to school with, was dead. Cedric had visited Werarra, had stayed here, when he and his grandfather were young men, when his grandmother was alive and making the place a home. The house had deteriorated, he'd told him. There were no separate living quarters, but if Alex was happy to do it tough...

Alex himself...*herself*...had emailed back saying tough was fine.

What now? He didn't even have a working bathroom. Asking a guy to use the outhouse was a stretch, *but a woman*?

He could fix the bathroom. Maybe. But not tonight.

And he still didn't want a woman. The women in his life had caused him nothing but grief and anguish. To have another, sharing his house, sharing his life...

Stop it with the dramatisation, he told himself harshly. She wouldn't want to stay even if he wanted her to. She obviously had a romantic view of what an outback Australian horse stud would be. One look at the outside privy and she'd run.

He didn't blame her.

Meanwhile...

Meanwhile he needed to feed her. He hurled sausages into the pan, sliced onions as if he could get rid of his anger on the chopping board, tossed them on top of the sausages and fumed. At himself more than her. He shouldn't have tried to employ anyone until he had this place decent, *but a woman*?

She took one look at the outside privy and wanted to die.

There was an inside bathroom, but... 'Plumbing's blocked,' Jack had said curtly, as he showed her her bedroom. 'Tree roots. Use the outhouse. There's a torch.'

The outhouse was fifty yards from the back door. A massive, overgrown rose almost hid it from view, and she had to make her way through a tunnel of vine to reach it.

A couple of hefty beef cattle were hanging their heads

over the fence, dripping water in the rain, looking at her as if she was an alien.

That's how she felt. Alien.

She locked the outhouse door, and something scrabbled over the outhouse's tin roof. What?

She wanted to go home.

'You're a big girl,' she told herself, out loud so whatever it was on the roof would get the picture. 'You need to get in there, front Jack Sexist Connor, find something to eat, get some sleep and then find a way out of this mess.'

The rain had eased for a minute, which was why she'd taken the chance and run out here. It started again, sheeting in under the door.

'I want to go home,' she wailed, and the thing on the roof stilled and listened.

And didn't answer.

He was cooking sausages. Eight fat sausages, Wombat Siding butcher's finest. He cooked mashed potato and boiled up some frozen peas to go with them.

He set the table with two knives, two forks, a ketchup bottle and two mugs. What more could a man want?

A woman might want more, he conceded, but she wasn't getting more.

What did he know about what a woman would want? A woman who was supposed to be a man.

She pushed open the door, and his thoughts stopped dead.

She'd been wearing black pants and a tailored wool jacket when she arrived. Her hair had been twisted into a knot. She'd been wearing red ankle boots, with old-fashioned buttons. She'd looked straight out of New York.

Now...

He'd left a pitcher and basin in her bedroom and she'd

obviously made use of it. She'd washed—the tendrils of blond curls around her face were damp—and her face was shiny clean with no hint of make-up. She was wearing jeans and an oversize sweater. Her curls hung free to her shoulders.

She was wearing thick, pink socks.

The résumé she'd sent said she was twenty-five years old. Right now she looked about sixteen. Pretty. Really pretty. Also…scared?

Daniel in the lion's den.

Or woman in Werarra.

Same thing, only he wasn't a lion. But she couldn't stay here.

'Sit down and wrap yourself round something to eat,' he said roughly, trying to hold to anger.

'Thank you.' She sidled into a chair on the far side of the table to him, still looking scared.

'Three sausages?'

'One.'

'Suit yourself.' He put one sausage onto a chipped plate, added a pile of mash and a heap of peas and put it in front of her. He ladled himself more.

He sat and started eating.

She sat and stared at her plate.

'What?' he said.

'I didn't lie,' she said in a small voice.

'I have the documentation,' he said, pointing to the pile of papers he'd left on the end of the table. '*My son.* That would be a male.'

'Nothing in any of my emails to you said I was a guy.'

'They didn't have to. I already knew. Your father's letter. The visa application. My son, the letter said. Plus Alexander. It's a guy's name.'

'Yes,' she said, and shoved her plate back. 'It is.'

'So?'

'My father doesn't get on with my older brother.' She was speaking calmly, in a strangely dull voice, like she'd reached some point and gone past. 'I've never figured why, but there's nothing anyone can do to fix it. I have two older sisters, and by the time I arrived Dad was desperate for a male heir other than Matt. He was sure I'd be the longed-for son. He planned on calling me Alexander, after his dad, only of course I ended up being Alexandra. So Dad filled in the birth certificate. Maybe he'd had a few drinks. Maybe it was just a slip, or maybe it was anger that I wasn't what he wanted. I don't know, but officially I'm Alexander. My family calls me Alexandra but on official stuff, I need to use Dad's spelling.' She tilted her chin and tried to glare at him. 'So...does it matter?'

'Yes,' he said flatly. 'It does. Your father said you were his son. I want to know why he lied.'

'He made a mistake.'

'Fathers don't make that sort of mistake.'

'They do if they always wanted their daughter to be a boy,' she said dully. She closed her eyes and clenched her fists. 'They do if they have Alzheimer's.'

Silence.

Whatever he'd expected, it wasn't that. The word hung. She hadn't wanted to say it, he thought. Admitting your dad was ill... It hurt, he thought. It hurt a lot.

Anger faded. He felt...cruel. Like he'd damaged something.

'So why does it matter?' she demanded, hauling herself together with a visible effort. 'What have you got against women?'

'Nothing.'

'I applied for jobs after graduating,' she said. 'I want horse work. To work with horses, not ponies, not pets. You try and get a job on a horse ranch when you're twenty-five and blonde and cute.'

And she said the word *cute* with such loathing he almost smiled.

'I can imagine…'

'No, you can't,' she snapped. 'You're six feet tall, built like a tank and you're male. You know nothing at all about what it's like to want to handle yourself with horses. This job…six months at Werarra Stud…is supposed to give me credibility with the ranchers back home, but you're just the same as every redneck cowboy know-all who ever told me I can't do it because I'm a girl.'

'So you're prepared to put up with an outhouse for six months?' he demanded, bemused.

'Not if it comes with an arrogant, chauvinistic oaf of an employer. And not if I have to eat grease.' And she shoved her plate across the table at him with force.

He caught it. He piled the sausage and mash absently onto his plate. He thought *cute* was a really good description.

Don't go there. This was a mistake he had to get rid of. He did not want to think any woman was cute.

'So you'll go home tomorrow,' he said, and she looked around and he thought if she had another plateful she might just possibly throw it at him.

'Why should I? I didn't lie about this job. You did.'

'I didn't.'

'Liar.'

'I told you it'd be rough.'

'I assumed you meant no shops. Living in the outback. The house… On the website it looks gorgeous.'

'That picture was taken eighty years ago. Romantic old homestead.'

'It's false advertising.'

'I'm not advertising my house,' he said evenly. 'I'm advertising my horses. I wanted the website to show a sense of history, that Werarra workhorses are part of what this country is.'

'Show the picture of your outhouse, then,' she snapped. 'Very historic.'

'You'll starve if you don't eat.'

'I couldn't eat sausages if you paid me.'

'Don't tell me—you're vegan.'

'I'm not.'

'Then why…'

'Because I've travelled for three days straight,' she snapped. 'Because I'm jet-lagged and overtired and overwrought. Because if you must know, my stomach is tied in knots and I'd like a dainty cucumber sandwich and a cup of weak tea with honey. Not a half-ton of grease. But if I have to go to bed with nothing, I will.' She shoved back her chair and stood. 'Good night.'

'Alex…'

'What?' she snapped.

'Sit down.'

'I don't want—'

'You don't want sausages,' he said and sighed, and opened the oven door of the great, old-fashioned fire stove that took up half the kitchen wall. He shoved his plate in there. 'I'll keep mine hot while I make you something you can eat.'

'Cucumber sandwiches?'

He had to smile. She sounded almost hopeful.

'Nope,' he said. 'I clean forgot cucumber on my shopping list. But sit down, shut up, and we'll see if we can find an alternative.'

She sat.

She looked up at him, half distrustful, half hopeful, and he felt something inside him twist.

Sophie, bleak as death, stirring her food with disinterest. *'I can't eat, Jack....'*

Sophie.

Do not think this woman is cute. Do not think this woman is anything other than a mistake you need to get rid of.

But for tonight... Yeah, she was needy. The explanation for the mix-up...it had hurt her to tell him about her dad; he could see that it hurt. And she was right, it shouldn't matter that she was a woman.

It wasn't her fault that it did. That the thought of a woman sitting on the far side of the table, a woman who even looked a little like Sophie, stirred something inside him that hurt. A lot.

She wasn't saying anything. He poured boiling water over a tea bag, and ladled in honey. He handed her the mug and watched her cradle it as if she needed its comfort.

The stove was putting out gentle warmth. This room was the only place in the house that bore the least semblance to cosy.

She didn't look cosy. She looked way out of her depth.

He was being cruel. If she was leaving in the morning, it wouldn't hurt to look after her.

He eyed her silently for a moment while she cradled her mug and stared at the battered wood of the ancient kitchen table.

It wouldn't hurt.

She was so spaced, so disoriented, that if she'd crashed down on the surface of the table she wouldn't be surprised. She felt light-headed, weird. When had she last eaten? On the plane this morning? Last night? When was last night and this morning? They were one and the same thing.

She wasn't making sense, even to herself. She should make herself stand up, head back to her allotted bedroom and go to sleep. And then get out of here.

Instead she cradled her mug of hot tea and stared at the worn surface of the table and did nothing.

She wasn't all that sure her legs would let her do anything else.

Jack was at the stove. He had his back to her. She wasn't sure what he was doing and she didn't care.

She'd wanted this so badly....

Why?

Veterinary Science hadn't been a problem for her. She'd dreamed of taking care of horses since she was a child. She'd put her head down and worked, and she'd succeeded.

Getting a job, though, was a sight harder. Horse medicine was hard, physically tough. The guys in college who were good at it were those who came from farms, who were built tough and big, who knew how to handle themselves. But she'd done it. She'd trained in equestrian care, she'd proved she could do what the guys did; she used brains instead of brawn, got fast at avoiding flying hooves, learned a bit of horse whispering.

It worked until she hit the real world, the world of employment, when no rancher wanted a five-feet-four-inch, willow-thin, blonde, twenty-five-year-old girl vet.

Like this guy didn't want her.

Her dad had organised this job for her. She'd been humiliated that she'd had to sink to using family connections, and now it seemed even family connections weren't enough.

What now?

Go back to New York? Find herself a nice little job caring for Manhattan pets? Her mother would be delighted.

Her dad?

He loved that she was a vet. He loved it that she wanted to treat horses.

He'd have loved it better if she was a son.

'Let's see if this suits you better,' Jack said, and slid another plate in front of her.

She looked—and looked again.

No sausages. Instead she was facing a small, fine china plate, with a piece of thin, golden toast, cut into four neat triangles. On the side was one perfectly rounded, perfectly poached egg.

She stared down at the egg and it was as much as she could do not to burst into tears.

'You're beat,' he said gently. 'Eat that and get to bed. Things will look better in the morning.'

She looked up at him, stunned by this gesture. This plate...it was like invalid cooking, designed to appeal to someone with the most jaded appetite. Where had this man...?

'Don't mind me, but I'm going back to my sausages,' he said, and hauled them out of the oven and did just that.

She'd thought she was too upset to eat, that she'd gone past hunger. He stayed silent, concentrating on his own meal. Left to herself, she managed to clean her plate.

He made her a second mug of tea. She finished that, too. She wasn't feeling strong enough to speak, to argue, to think about the situation she was in. She'd sleep, she thought. Then...then...

'There's not a lot I can't do that a guy can do,' she said, not very coherently but it was the best she could manage at the end of the meal.

'No,' he said. 'But you wouldn't want to stay here.'

'Neither would any male vet I trained with.'

He nodded. 'I shouldn't have let anyone come.'

'You need me, why?'

'I don't need you.'

'Right,' she said, and rose. 'I guess that's it, then. Maybe I should say thank-you for the egg but I won't. I've just paid the airfare to come halfway round the world for a job that doesn't exist. Compared to that…well, it does seem an egg is pretty lousy wages.'

CHAPTER TWO

THE bedroom was a faded approximation to her dreams. It had once been beautiful, large and gracious, with gorgeous flowered wallpaper, rich, tasselled drapes, a high ceiling, wide windows and a bed wide enough to fit three of her. It still was beautiful—sort of. She could ignore the faded wallpaper, the shredded drapes. For despite the air of neglect and decay, her bed was made up with clean, crisp linen. The mattress and pillows were surprisingly soft. Magically soft.

Soft enough that despite her emotional upheaval, despite the fact that it was barely seven o'clock, she was asleep as soon as her head touched the pillow.

But reality didn't go away. She woke up with a jolt in the small hours, and remembered where she was, and remembered her life was pretty much over.

Okay, maybe she was exaggerating, she decided, as she stared bleakly into the darkness. She had the money to have a holiday. She could go back to Sydney, do some sightseeing, head back to New York and tell everyone she'd been conned.

Her friends had been derisive when she'd told them what she was doing. 'You? On an outback station? Man-of-all-work as well as vet for stockhorses? Get real, Alex, you're too blonde.'

The teasing had been good-natured but she'd heard the serious incredulity behind it. No one would be surprised when she came home.

And then what? Her thoughts were growing bleaker. If this low-life cowboy kicked her off this farm…

He didn't have to kick her off. There was no way she'd stay here, with this ramshackle house, without a bathroom, with his chauvinistic attitudes.

Bleak-R-Us.

The silence was deafening. She was used to city sounds, city lights filtering through the drapes. Here, there was nothing.

If there was nothing, she had to leave.

Okay. She could do what her mother wanted, she thought. Concede defeat. Get a job caring for New York's pampered pooches. Her mother had all sorts of contacts who could get her such a job. Unlike her dad, who'd loved the idea of her working with horses, and who'd used the only contact he had. Which just happened to be forty years out of date.

And for a son, not for a daughter.

Her thoughts were all over the place, but suddenly she was back with her dad. Why did it make a difference? She'd never been able to figure why her dad wasn't happy with the son he had; why he'd been desperate to have another.

Like she couldn't figure why it was so important to Jack Connor that she was male.

He'd cooked her an egg.

It was a small thing. In the face of his boorish behaviour it was inconsequential, yet somehow it made a difference.

He was used to invalid cookery, she thought. Maria had made meals like that for her when she was ill. The fact that Jack had done it…

It meant nothing. One egg does not a silk purse make. He was still, very much, a sow's ear. A sow's ear she'd be seeing the last of tomorrow morning. Or this morning.

She checked her watch: 3:00 a.m. Four hours before she could stalk away from this place and never come back.

Admit defeat?

Yes, she told her pillow. Yes, because she had no choice.

She rolled over in bed and saw a flicker of light behind the curtains.

Jack, heading for the outhouse?

The outhouse was on the other side of the house.

Someone was out there.

So what? She shoved her pillow over her head and tried to sleep.

It was midday in Manhattan. She was wide awake.

The light.

Ignore it. Go to sleep.

Her legs were twitchy. She'd spent too long on too many planes.

So what? Go to sleep.

Or what?

Sancha was one of the stud's prize mares. This was her second foaling. He hadn't expected trouble.

At two-thirty he'd known things were happening but the signs were normal. He'd checked the foal had a nice healthy heartbeat. He'd brought in thick fresh straw, then sat back and waited. Foaling was normally explosively fast. Horses usually delivered within half an hour.

She didn't.

She was in trouble.

So was the foal. The presentation was all wrong. The heartbeat was becoming erratic.

He need a vet. Now.

He had one in the house. But…

He wasn't all that sure he trusted her credentials. Besides, he'd sacked her. He could hardly ask her to help.

But if he didn't…it'd take an hour to get the local vet here and that heartbeat meant he didn't have an hour.

He swallowed his pride and thought, Thank heaven he'd made the girl an egg.

She hauled on her fleecy bathrobe and headed out to the veranda. Just to see. Just because staying in bed was unbearable. She could see lightning in the distance but the storm was past. It had stopped raining. The air felt cool and crisp and clean. She needed cool air to clear her head.

She walked out the back door, and barrelled straight into Jack.

He caught her, steadied her, but it took a moment longer for her breath to steady. He was so big…. It was the middle of the night. This place was creepy.

He was big.

'Are you really a vet?' he demanded, and she stiffened and hauled away.

'Does it matter?'

'Yes,' he said curtly. 'I've a mare with dystocia. She's been labouring for at least an hour and nothing's happened. I can't get the presentation right—there are hooves everywhere. I'll lose her.'

'My vet bag's in the car,' she snapped. 'Get it and show me where she is.'

She was cute, blonde, female. She was wearing a pink, fuzzy bathrobe.

She was a veterinarian.

From the time she entered the stables, her entire attention was on the mare. He was there only to answer curt questions she snapped at him as she examined her.

'How long since you found her? Was she distressed then? Has she foaled before?'

'With no problem. I'm sure it's the presentation. I can't fix it.'

She hauled off her bathrobe, shoved her arm in the bucket of soapy water and performed a fast double-check. She didn't trust him.

Why should she?

The mare was deeply distressed. She'd been moving round, agitated, lying, rolling, standing again. Alex moved with her as she examined her, not putting herself at risk but doing what had to be done, fast.

Her examination was swift, and so was her conclusion.

'After an hour's labour, there's no way we'll get it out naturally from the position it's in and it's too risky to try and manoeuvre it. The alternative's a caesarean, but I'd need help and I'd need equipment.'

'I have equipment and I can help,' he said steadily, but he was thinking, Did he have enough? And...*to do a caesarean, here?* He knew the drill. What they needed was an equipped surgery, sterile environs, equipment and drugs to make this possible. Even the thought of moving the mare and holding her seemed impossible. If he had another strong guy...

He had a petite blonde, in a cute bathrobe.

But she hadn't seemed to notice that she was totally unsuited for the job at hand. She was checking the beams overhead.

'Are you squeamish?'

What, him? 'No,' he snapped, revolted.

'I'd need ropes and more water. I'd need decent lights.

I'd need warmed blankets—get a heater out here, anything. Just more of it. What sort of equipment are you talking?'

'I hope we have everything you need,' he told her, and led her swiftly out to the storeroom at the back of the stables.

The Wombat Siding vet had equipped the store. With over a hundred horses, the vet was out here often, so he'd set up a base here. Three hours back to fetch equipment wasn't possible so he'd built a base here.

And Alex's eyes lit at the sight of the stuff he had. She didn't hesitate. She started hauling out equipment and handing it to him.

'So far, so good,' she said curtly. 'With this gear it might just be possible. You realise I'm only aiming to save the mare. You know foal survival under these conditions is barely ten percent.'

'I know that.'

'You won't faint?'

'No.'

'I've seen tougher cowboys than you faint, but you faint and your mare dies. Simple as that. I can't do it alone.'

'I'm with you every step of the way.'

She stared at him long and hard, and then gave a brisk nod, as if he'd passed some unseen test.

'Right,' she snapped. 'Let's do it.'

It was hard, it was risky.

She was skilled.

She whispered to the mare. Administered the anaesthetic. Guided her down.

Together they rolled her into position, and he was stunned at the strength of her. She didn't appear to notice how much strength it took.

With the mare unconscious she set up a drip. She'd

teamed with Jack to rope the mare into position, using the beams above, but Jack still needed to support her. He was told to supervise the ventilator delivering oxygen plus the drip administering electrolytes and fluids.

She delivered curt instructions and he followed. This was her call.

There was no choice. If she wasn't here, he'd lose the mare. Simple as that.

She was a vet.

She was wearing a pink bathrobe. She'd tugged her hair back with a piece of hay twine. She shouldn't look professional.

She looked totally professional.

She was clipping the hair from the mare's abdomen, fast, sure, then doing a speedy sterile prep. Checking instruments. Looking to him for reassurance.

'Ready?'

'I'm ready,' he said, and wondered if he was.

He had to be.

He watched, awed, as she made a foot-long incision in the midline of the abdomen, then made an incision into the uterus giving access to the foal.

'Say your prayers,' she said, and hauled out a tiny hoof, and then another.

This was a big mare. The foal was small, but compared to this young woman... For her to lift it free...

He made a move to help her.

'Watch that oxygen,' she snapped. 'Leave this to me. It's mare first, foal second.'

He understood. Emergency caesareans in horses rarely meant a live foal. They were all about saving the life of the mare.

If the airway he was monitoring blocked, they'd lose the mare, so he could only watch as she lifted the foal free. She staggered a little under the weight, but he knew enough now not to offer to help. She steadied, checked, put her face against its nuzzle, then carried it across to the bed of straw where he'd laid blankets. He'd started a blow heater, directing it to the blankets, to make it warm.

Just in case...

Maybe there was a case.

He kept doing what he was doing, but he had space to watch as she swiftly cleared its nose, inserted the endotracheal tube he'd hardly noticed she'd set up, started oxygen, then returned briskly to the mare. All in the space of seconds. She couldn't leave the mare for any longer.

The foal was totally limp. But...

'There's a chance,' she said, returning fast to the job at hand. There was no time, no manpower, to care for the foal more than she'd done.

She had to stitch the wound closed. He had to stay where he was, supporting the mare, keeping the airway clear.

But he watched the foal out of the corner of his eye. Saw faint movement.

The mare shifted, an involuntary, unconscious shudder.

'Watch her,' Alex ordered. 'You want to risk both?'

No. He went back to what he was doing. Making sure she was steady. Making sure she lived.

Alex went back to stitching.

He watched her blond, bent head and he felt awed. He thought back to the sausages and outhouse and felt...stupid.

And cruel.

This woman had come halfway round the world so she could have a chance to do what she was doing brilliantly. And he'd begrudged her an egg.

There was no time for taking this further now, though. With the stitching closed, she removed the ropes. He helped her shove fresh straw under the mare's side, then manoeuvred her into lateral recumbency, on her side.

The foal...

'Watch her,' she said again, more mildly this time, and she left him to the mare and stooped back over the foal.

'We still have him,' she said, in a voice that said it mattered. Her voice held surprise and a little awe. She checked more thoroughly and he saw the foal stir and shift. *'Her,'* Alex corrected herself, and there was no concealing the emotion she felt. 'Let's get the birth certificate right on this one.'

A filly. Out of Sancha.

If he got a live mare and foal out of this night... He couldn't describe the feeling.

But it wasn't certain yet. She was setting up an IV line, then using more blankets to towel the foal. It...*she*...was still limp.

Everything had to go right with a foaling. Foals didn't survive premature delivery. They seldom survived caesareans. To get a good outcome...

Please...

Sancha stirred under his hands, whinnied, lifted her head.

'Hey.' He laid his head on her head, the way he used to do as a kid, the way his grandfather had taught him. His grandfather was a cruel drunk, mean to everything and everyone but his horses, but Jack had watched him and learned, and the skills were there when he needed them. 'There's no need to get up,' he whispered to her. 'Your baby's in good hands.'

She was.

They watched and waited. There seemed nothing of the Manhattan princess about Alex right now. She had all the time in the world, all the patience.

Jack whispered to his mare, watched his foal—and watched this woman who'd transformed before his eyes.

Finally the foal started to struggle, starting to search for her feet. Alex helped her up, a wobbly tangle of spindly legs and huge head, and Jack felt...felt...

Like a horseman shouldn't feel. He didn't get emotional. He didn't care?

The foal whinnied and the mare responded. She struggled, as well, and Alex was suddenly back with him. The mare rose, as unsteady as her daughter, but finally with their help she was upright.

She turned and nosed her daughter. The foal whinnied in response, and started magically to nose underneath her.

Alex smiled and smiled. She guided the foal to the teat and then stood back.

'I think we might just have won,' she whispered, and Jack might have been struggling to hide his emotions but Alex surely wasn't. Tears were tracking down her cheeks and he felt an almost irresistible urge to wipe them for her.

He watched her. He watched the foal and the sensations were indescribable. The urge to hug this woman, to lift her and spin her in triumph, to share this amazing feeling...

It had to be suppressed—of course it did—but nothing had ever been harder.

So she wiped her tears herself, swiping her bathrobe sleeve over her face, sniffing, smiling through tears, then started to clear away the stained straw. Moving on. Being sensible.

More sensible than him.

'She'll need to be kept quiet for weeks,' she said, trying to sound brusque rather than emotional—but not succeeding. 'This isn't like a human caesarean—all her innards are bearing down on those stitches. The foal will need exercise, though. It's imperative to allow her to run and frolic, so it'll be hand-walking the mare every day while her baby has her runs.'

She'd started loading her gear back into her bag. 'That's more work for you,' she said, still brusque. Not looking at him. 'A lot of extra work. You might need to think about finding extra help. Seeing as you've sacked me.'

She might not be looking at him, but he was looking at her. She was wearing a bloodstained and filthy bathrobe. Her hair was flying every which way.

He'd never seen anything more beautiful in his life.

Which was the sort of thing he needed to stop thinking if he was offering her a job.

He was offering her a job. He had no choice. He'd treated her appallingly and she'd replied by saving his mare and foal.

'The indoor bathroom drain only blocked last week,' he told her before he could let prudence, sense, anything, hold sway. 'I can pay priority rates and arrange a plumber to come this morning. We should have an operating bathroom by dusk. For now, though... The boiler in the outside laundry is full of hot water. I can cart water into the bath so you can get yourself clean.'

She stilled and stared at him. 'Hot water?' she whispered, as if he was offering the Holy Grail.

'Yes.'

'You're offering me a bath?'

'And a job.'

'Forget jobs, just give me a bath,' she said, breathing deeply. She straightened and looked at him full-on, as if reading his face for truth. 'A great big, hot, gorgeous bath? I'll cart the water myself if I must.'

'No more carting for you tonight,' he said gruffly. 'You've done enough. About this job...'

'Tomorrow,' she said. 'I'll think about anything you like, as long as the bath comes first.'

She headed for her bath. The ancient claw-foot tub was huge and it took a while to fill but she beamed the whole time he filled it. He made sure she had everything she needed, then headed back out to the stables.

He watched over his mare and foal and thought about what had just happened.

He'd arrived here after Sophie's death thinking he had a manager and a stablehand. The stablehand had been yet one more instance of his manager's fraudulent account-ing. So had the costs he'd billed Jack for, for the upkeep of the buildings. Seemingly his grandfather hadn't worried about infrastructure for years and his crook of a manager had made things worse. The horses had been cared for, the cattle had kept the grass down, but nothing else had been done to the place at all. Jack was therefore faced with no help and no place fit to house anyone to help him.

When Cedric Patterson's letter came he'd been pushed to the limit. Cedric's offer had been for a farmhand and a vet, rolled into one.

The manager's residence was uninhabitable and he didn't have time to fix it. But could he put a young man into the main house? A wide-eyed student, who needed experience to get a job elsewhere? Who'd shrugged off his assurance that this place was rough as if it was nothing? Such a kid might well take the job. Such a kid might not intrude too much on his life.

He'd mulled over the letter for a couple of days before replying but it had been too tempting to resist. Now it was even more tempting. Alex was *some* vet.

So, he'd offered her the job. If she accepted, the deci-sion was made.

Which meant living with her for six months.

He didn't want to live with anyone for six months, but he sat on a hay bale and watched mare and foal slowly recover from their ordeal, and he thought of Alex's skill and speed, and he knew this was a gift he couldn't knock back.

He thought of how he'd felt, watching her over the kitchen table. Remembering Sophie. Remembering pain. Those last few months as Sophie had spiralled into depression so great nothing could touch her were still raw and dreadful.

Alex had nothing to do with Sophie, he told himself harshly. All he had to do was stay aloof.

All he had to do was not to care. That was his promise to himself. Never to care again.

But she was lovely. And clever and skilled.

And gorgeous.

'Cut it out,' he growled, and his mare stirred in alarm. Her foal, however, kept right on drinking.

'See, that's what I need to be,' he told his beautiful mare. 'Single-minded, like your baby. I'm here to produce the best stockhorses in Australia and I'm interested in nothing else.'

Liar. He was very, very interested in the woman he'd just shown into the bathroom. He'd watched her face light when she'd seen the steaming bathtub of hot water and he'd wanted…he'd wanted…

It didn't matter what he wanted, he thought. He knew what he had to do.

He'd offered her a job. This stud needed her.

That was all it was. An employer/employee relationship, starting now.

If she stayed.

He shouldn't want her to stay—but he did.

* * *

Would she stay?

Did it matter?

She lay back in the vast, old-fashioned bathtub and let the hot water soothe her soul. Nothing mattered but this hot water.

And the fact that she'd saved a mare and foal. It was what she was trained to do and the outcome was deeply satisfying.

And the fact that Jack Connor had offered her a job?

She shouldn't take it. He was an arrogant, chauvinistic toad, she told herself. And this place was a dump.

Except...it wasn't. The stables were brilliant. The equipment Jack had, not just medical stuff but every single horse fitting, was first-class. He'd poured money into the stables, into the horses, rather than the house.

She could forgive a lot of a man who put his animals' needs before his own.

And he'd fix the bathroom. He'd promised. She could have a bath like this every night.

She wouldn't have to go home and do her mother's bidding.

She could stay...with Jack?

Maybe she needed a bit of cold water in this bath.

Whoa. That was exactly the sort of thing she didn't need to be thinking. Jack Connor was an arrogant man. The fact that he was drop-dead sexy, the fact that he'd smiled down at the foal and his smile made her toes curl...

Neither of those things could be allowed to matter.

Or both of those things should make her run a mile.

She shouldn't stay.

She poked one pink toe out of the water and surveyed it with care. She'd had her toenails painted before she left New York.

What was she thinking, getting her toenails painted to come here?

'Not to impress Jack Connor, that's for sure,' she told herself. 'If I stay here it'll be hobnail boots for the duration.'

Good. That was what she was here for. She was not here to impress Jack Connor.

She'd saved his mare and foal. She'd made that grim face break into a smile.

He'd made her an egg.

'You're a fool, Alex Patterson,' she told herself. 'Your father thinks of you as a boy. If you're going to stay here, you need to think of yourself as one, too. No interest in a very sexy guy.'

No?

No.

But her toe was still out of the water.

The toe was a symbol. Most of Alex Patterson was one very sensible vet. There was a tiny bit, though, that refused to be sensible.

There was a tiny bit remembering that smile.

CHAPTER THREE

SHE woke and it was eleven o'clock and someone was thumping outside her bedroom window.

Someones. Male voices.

She double-checked her clock—surely she hadn't slept so long. Her head didn't have a clue what time it was. Eleven in the morning—that'd make it...nine at night in Manhattan. She should be just going to bed.

She was wide awake. She crept over to the drapes and pushed one aside, a little bit. Expecting to see Jack.

A van was parked right by her bedroom window. Wombat Siding Plumbing, it said on this side. She could see three guys with shovels. Bathroom menders.

Jack might just be a man of his word, she thought, and grinned.

Where was he?

Did it matter? The sun was shining. The day was washed clean and delicious. Her bathroom was being prepared. How was her mare?

It took her all of two minutes to dress. She felt weirdly light-headed, tingling with the lighthearted feeling that this might work, that contrary to first impressions, here might be a veterinarian job she could get her teeth into.

And she'd be working beside a guy called Jack.

He wasn't in the kitchen. Instead she found a note.

Sorry, but you'll still need to use the outhouse this morning. Plumbing is promised by tonight. Help yourself to breakfast and go back to sleep. You deserve it. I'm working down the back paddock but am checking Sancha and her foal every couple of hours. They look great. Thank you.

There was nothing in that note to get excited about. Nothing to make this lighthearted frisson even more... tingly.

Except it did.

Go back to bed?

She'd thought she wanted to sleep until Monday. She was wrong.

Two pieces of toast and two mugs of strong coffee later—another plus, Jack obviously knew decent coffee—she headed out to the stables.

As promised, Sancha and her foal looked wonderful. The mare was a deep, dark bay, with white forelock and legs. Her foal was a mirror image. They looked supremely content. Sancha tolerated her checking her handiwork and she found no problem.

'I'll take you for a wee walk round the home paddock this afternoon,' she promised her. 'No exercise for you for a while but your baby needs it.'

Where was Jack?

She tuned out the sounds of the plumbers and listened. From below the house came the sounds of a chainsaw. Jack was working?

She should leave him to it.

Pigs might fly.

She headed towards the sound, following the creek just below the house. It really was the most stunning property, she thought. It had been cleared sympathetically, with massive river red gums still dotted across the landscape. A few hefty beef cattle grazed peacefully under the trees. They'd be used to keep the grass down, she thought, a necessity with such rich pasture. The country was gently undulating, with the high mountain peaks of the Snowies forming a magnificent backdrop. Last night's rain had washed the place clean, and every bird in the country seemed to be squawking its pleasure.

The Australian High Country. The internet had told her it'd be beautiful, and this time the web hadn't lied.

She rounded a bend in the creek—and saw something even more beautiful.

Jack. Stripped to his waist. Hauling logs clear from an ancient, long-dead tree, ready for cutting.

She stopped, stunned to breathlessness. She'd never seen a body so...ripped.

If she was a different sort of girl she might indulge in a maidenly swoon, she thought, and fought to recover.

He lifted his head and saw her—and he stilled.

'You're supposed to be sleeping.'

'I came here to work.'

'No more mares are foaling right now.'

'Thank heaven for that,' she said, and ventured a smile. Seeing if it'd work.

It didn't. He looked...disconcerted, she thought. As though he didn't know where to pigeonhole her.

As though he'd like her pigeonhole to be somewhere else.

She glanced around and saw a pile of chopped logs, neatly stacked on a trailer. There was an even bigger pile of non-stacked timber beside it.

She metaphorically spat on her hands, lifted a log and set it on the trailer.

'You can't do that.'

She heaved a second log onto the tractor and lifted another. 'Why not?'

'It's not your—'

'Job? Yes, it is. The agreement was I'd work as a vet and handyman.'

'Handy*man*,' he said, with something akin to loathing.

'Do we need to go there again?'

'No, but—'

'There you go, then,' she said, and smiled and kept on stacking.

How was a man supposed to work with a woman like this beside him?

He'd used the tractor to haul a dead tree out of the creek. Chopped, it'd provide a year's heating. The fire stove was nearly out. This needed doing.

Not with Alex.

She didn't know the rules. She was heaving timber as if she was his mate, rather than…

Rather than what? He was being a chauvinist. Hadn't he learned his lesson last night?

But the logs were far too heavy for a woman. Her hands…

She didn't want to be treated as a woman, he told himself. Her hands were her business.

No.

'If you were a guy, I'd still be saying put gloves on,' he growled. 'There's a heap up in the stables. Find your size and don't come back again until you have them on.'

'I don't need—'

'I'm your employer,' he snapped. 'I get to pay employee insurance. Gloves or you don't work.'

She straightened and stared at him. That stare might work on some, he thought, but it wasn't working on him.

'Your choice,' he said, and turned his chainsaw back on.

She glowered, then stomped up to the stables to fetch some gloves. And then came back and kept right on working.

They worked solidly for two hours, and Jack was totally disconcerted. He started chopping the logs a little smaller, to make it easier for her to stack, but he'd expected after half an hour she'd have long quitted.

She hadn't. She didn't.

He worked on. She piled the trailer high. He had to stop to take it up to the house and empty it. She followed the truck and trailer to the house and helped heave wood into the woodshed. Then, as he checked again on Sancha and the foal, without being asked, she took the tractor and headed back to the river to start on the next load.

Either she was stronger than she looked, or she was pig stubborn. He couldn't tell unless he could see her hands. He couldn't see her hands because she kept the gloves on. She worked with a steady rhythm he found disconcerting.

She was from New York. She shouldn't be able to heave wood almost as easily as he did.

She did.

Finally the second trailer was full.

Lunch.

He'd slapped a bit of beef into bread to make sandwiches to bring with him. He'd brought down beer.

There wasn't enough to go round, and it was time she stopped.

'There's heaps of food in the kitchen,' he told her. 'You've done a decent day's work. Head back up and get some rest.'

She shook her head. She'd been carrying a sweater when

she arrived. She'd laid it aside at the edge of the clearing. She went to it now, and retrieved a parcel from under it.

A water bottle and a packet of sandwiches. Neater than the ones he'd made.

'How did you know...?'

'You left the sandwich bread and the cutting board on the sink,' she said. 'It didn't take Einstein to figure sandwiches had been made. I figured if you were avoiding plumbers, I would, too.'

'I'm not avoiding plumbers.'

'Avoiding me, then? You want to tell me what you have against women?' She bit into her sandwich, making it a casual question. Like it didn't matter.

'I don't have anything against women. I just assumed you couldn't be up to the job.'

'And now you find I am,' she said, and looked at him and beamed—like he'd just given her the best of compliments

She was teasing him?

He smiled back. He had no choice in the face of that beam. 'More than up to the job,' he admitted. 'You made your full six months' wages last night. You can go home happy.'

'If I want to go home.'

'You want to stay?'

'Yes,' she said, and had a bit more sandwich. 'I have a reputation to make. Six months' hard work and a reference from Werarra at the end of it should see me set for a decent job back home. Mind, please don't update your website while I apply for jobs. This place is known internationally as a major stud. Seeing your outhouse would do your reputation no end of harm.'

'It's not the outhouse buyers are interested in. It's the horses.'

'Which is why you don't care for anything but?'

It was a question. She was waiting for an answer.

This was none of her business, he told himself. He didn't need to tell her anything.

But she was happily munching sandwiches she'd made herself. She'd worked hard all morning. She'd worked hard last night.

She'd come halfway round the world to take an appalling job.

'Werarra horses are some of the best stockhorses in the world,' he said, trying to keep emotion out of what he needed to tell her. 'Maybe they're the best. Since my grandmother died, my grandfather hasn't cared for anything but the horses, but he has cared for them.'

'My brother checked this place out for me on the internet,' she said conversationally. 'He says your grandpa died last year but the place has been run by a manager. You're the owner but you've not been near the place. You've been heading an IT company.'

'I've also been caring for my sister.'

Why had he said that? It had sounded like an explosion. It was an explosion.

She'd heard it for what it was. Her slight, teasing expression faded.

'She's dead,' she said, and it wasn't a question.

'She died,' he said, tight and hard. 'Black depression and its consequences. I couldn't care enough.'

'I'm sure you did,' she said softly. 'I can imagine just how much you cared, and I'm so sorry.'

She looked up toward the house. Three mares were standing on the hillside looking down at them. Their coats glistening in the midday sun. They looked perfectly groomed, perfectly cared for, perfect.

Sophie's death seemed a raised sword over their heads. He shouldn't have told her.

She shouldn't have instinctively understood, but he knew that she did.

'You learned to look after horses in your childhood?' she asked him, and he heard the slight softening in her tone, which, he thought, was all she was offering in the way of sympathy. He didn't even want that. Why had he told her? 'Here?'

'Here,' he snapped. He'd told her too much.

'Your grandfather taught you?'

'I watched him,' he said, and he knew by her expression that she'd heard the difference.

'And after his death you let the manager run the place until your sister died.'

'Yes,' he said, practically grinding his teeth. How did this woman know?

'So now, you've had time to get the horses up to scratch, but not the house,' she said briskly, and he needed to sound brisk, too. She was simply taking in information and moving on. Not getting emotional.

How rare was that in a woman? How rare was that in anyone?

'The house doesn't matter,' he told her.

'It does if it has tree roots in the sewer,' she said darkly. 'It does if I'm staying. I need new curtains for my bedroom. The plumbers nearly had a ringside seat this morning.'

He smiled. Emotion was done with. She was back to being bolshie again. Assertive.

Cute.

'I'll find you curtains,' he promised.

'Right,' she said. 'You want to get this wood done?'

For answer he leaned across and flicked off one of her gloves.

She tugged away but she couldn't tug fast enough. He took her hand and tugged open her fingers, exposing her palm.

Three blisters. Broken. Raw.

He knew it. She was a kid from Manhattan who'd just finished vet school. She played tough but she lied.

'Enough,' he said. 'Alex, enough.'

'I want this job.' It was a whisper, and suddenly emotion was out there, front and centre. 'You can't know how much I want this job.'

'Then toughen up,' he said, staring down at the raw, exposed skin. 'And you don't do that by hurling yourself into work like a bull at the gate. You do it by starting gradually and working up. By the end of six months you'll be hurling wood like the best of them. For now, take yourself back to the house, clean your hands up and rest.'

'I—'

'Just do it.'

She looked up at him.

Mistake.

She was too close. Too near. Her eyes were darkly shadowed—jet lag must be coming into play, as well as last night's drama. She looked too pale, too small. Her hand was in his.

She was looking at him like she was caught. Which was how he felt. Caught.

He did not want…

A rustle in the bushes caught his attention. Actually, anything would have caught his attention. He was desperate for his attention to be caught.

He dropped her hand and swivelled.

Oliver.

He knew this kid, the son of the previous manager. He was Brian's oldest, eleven years old. He was undersized for his age, freckled, his spiky, strawberry-red hair unbrushed and uncared for, too skinny, a bit bedraggled and as shy as the most nervous of his young horses.

He'd been his father's shadow when Jack first returned to the farm. His dad disappeared and so had Oliver, but for the past few weeks he'd seen him back here, on and off. He was a shadow in the undergrowth, silently watching him.

The last time he'd seen him, he'd managed to corner him and send him home. Kindly but firmly. He didn't want a kid around horses three times as big as he was. Jack couldn't be everywhere. To have the kid wandering the farm was dangerous.

He'd dropped in on Brenda—Brian's abandoned wife— and told her to keep an eye on her son. Told her to keep him away from the farm, away from the horses.

She'd told him the kid wasn't hers. He was the product of one of Brian's earlier relationships. She was stuck with him, caring for him as best she could, but with two small girls of her own she couldn't be expected to watch him all the time.

He'd been dismayed, but there was nothing he could do. 'Just keep him off my property,' he'd said. But regardless, the kid was in the bushes, watching them. He knew he shouldn't be here. As Jack saw him, he backed and looked like he'd run.

'Hey,' Alex said, before he could say a word. 'You're the kid who showed me where to come yesterday. Thank you. Would you like a sandwich?'

That was pretty much the opposite of what Jack had planned to say. He opened his mouth to tell him to leave, but Alex had already bounced up. 'Beef or jam,' she said. 'Nothing fancy. Jam's good.'

The kid was out of the bushes like he'd been grabbed and pulled. He had a sandwich in his hand, in his mouth, before Jack could say a word.

Alex grinned. 'I do like a guy who appreciates home cooking,' she said. 'What's your name?'

'Oliver.' Through sandwich.

'I'm pleased to meet you, Oliver.' She glanced to Jack. 'Is this a friend of yours?'

How to explain the connection? Son of an ex-manager who'd run off with another woman and a whole lot of money that rightfully belonged to the farm. Not possible.

'Oliver's mum owns the next-door property,' he said tightly.

That wasn't exactly true either. He owned the next-door property. Brenda was staying there free.

If he could kick Brenda out he might be able to fill it with a decent farm worker, but Brian had robbed Brenda, too. He didn't have the heart to evict her.

But he did not want this kid here. This kid whose neediness made him think of another child... Sophie's eyes, looking at him through Oliver.

'Your mum'll be worried,' he said to Oliver. Curtly.

'Brenda knows where I am.'

'She knows I don't like you here.'

'But I can help,' Oliver said, and grabbed another sandwich. 'With the horses. I want to.'

And once again, Alex beat him in responding. 'Maybe you can,' she said, watching him attack his sandwich like he hadn't eaten for days. 'We had a foal last night. You want to see? I'm about to take her mum out for a gentle walk in the home paddock. Would you like to help before you go home?'

'Yes,' Oliver said, but with a nervous look at Jack.

'Let's go, then,' Alex said. She glanced at Jack. 'I assume you have no objection if I take her out? It's what the vet recommends.'

'Oliver should be in school.'

'Saturday,' Oliver said, as if he was dumb.

Which pretty much summed up how he was feeling. Dumb. Or out of control.

He owned this stud. He did not want this woman here. He did not want this kid here.

'He'll be gone in a couple of hours,' Alex said, as if she could read his mind. 'You're stuck with me, though. Come on, Oliver, let's get our work done.'

'Your hands…' he said.

'I'll clean them first,' she said. 'Oliver can help me.'

'I'd rather help Jack,' Oliver said, and Jack thought that was exactly what the trouble was. Brenda was a mess; it was all she could do to cope with her four- and two-year-old. She was brusquely kind to Oliver but Oliver needed more.

There was no way Jack could go down that road. He helped Brenda financially. He let her stay in the house and that was an end to it.

'Help Alex if you like,' he growled. 'Do what you like as long as you let me be.'

Women… Children… He wanted nothing to do with either of them.

CHAPTER FOUR

SHE led Sancha out of the stalls. The gangly foal wobbled gamely behind her mother, with Oliver beaming by her side like a proud uncle. They walked at a snail's pace.

If Alex had her druthers she'd have kept Sancha confined for the next four weeks. The pressure on her stitches was enormous, but if the foal was to develop, she had to figure what grass was, what running was. Alex's job was to keep Sancha safe while the foal learned to be a foal.

Out in the paddock, Sancha raised her gorgeous velvety nose to the sun, as if she intended to soak up every ray.

'Will you let her go?' Oliver breathed.

'No. She has stitches across her tummy. She's not allowed to stretch them.' She hesitated, seeing the little boy's yearning face. She remembered, years ago, her father taking her to a friend's ranch. She'd been about the same age as Oliver. Her dad's friend had let her muck out the stables, and had taught her to groom.

Just touching horses…being with them…

She knew that longing, and she was seeing it now.

'Would you like to hold her?' she asked. 'You need to keep her very still.'

'Yes,' Oliver breathed, and took the bridle and held it like he was holding diamonds. 'He doesn't let me,' he said.

'He?'

'Jack. Dad used to let me help but now he's gone and Jack says I shouldn't come here any more.' He said it in the same tones as if announcing the end of the world. 'Brenda says it's no wonder. She says Dad robbed us blind and he robbed Jack, too. She says it's amazing he still lets us live here, and to leave him alone. But I used to ride Cracker. He's old and he's great but Jack's put him in the back paddock, and I really, really miss him.'

He sniffed, and Alex felt like sniffing, too. And she thought, What had this kid done to make Jack prevent him from being with the horse he so obviously loved?

'Can I have another sandwich before I go home?' the little boy asked.

'Yes,' she said, thinking she might just be heading for conflict here.

One needy kid.

Jack was her boss. She needed to be deferential.

Deferential wasn't in her nature. One sandwich? Jack was going to have to do better than that.

Jet lag was insidious. One minute she was wide awake, the next she was dead on her feet. Oliver left and she headed for bed. She woke and the sun was slipping behind the mountains. A weird bird was cackling in the gums outside her bedroom window. The breeze was making the faded drapes flutter, and she lay in bed and thought of the winter she'd left in Manhattan and she decided this could work.

Then she thought of Jack Connor and thought maybe not.

And not because he was arrogant. There was something about him....

Actually, there was a lot about him. She'd gone through vet school with testosterone-driven guys. Her college had organised her work experience on some decent ranches and she'd met some pretty hot men.

They hadn't pushed her buttons like Jack Connor did. She lay and sleepily thought of him, and her buttons were definitely pushed.

It was jet lag, she told herself. Lack of sleep and changing time zones would make any woman susceptible to the hunk that Jack Connor was.

He was arrogant. He was a chauvinist.

And he didn't let Oliver help with the horses.

On that idea she thrust back the covers. Hold the thought, she told herself. Arrogant, chauvinist and unkind. If she could hold on to that for six months, then she could do this job.

Please...

She headed for the kitchen. He was cooking. Sausages. Again. Terrific.

Be grateful he's cooking anything, she told herself. With this guy, it was a wonder he hadn't handed her an apron and a dishcloth the moment she walked in the door.

But sausages...

'I had chicken for a casserole,' he said before she could open her mouth. 'It seems to have disappeared. As does an entire piece of cold roast beef, the apple pie I bought yesterday and half our weekly fruit rations. That was some bedtime snack.'

'I gave it to Oliver,' she said, and watched him still.

'What gives you the right—'

'Take it out of my wages.' She tilted her chin and met his glare head-on.

'Don't encourage him.'

'He seems to be starving.'

'He's not starving. His mother's on the pension. I give her free rent. There's enough for food.'

'He's still starving.'

'He's not my business.' It was like an explosion, and she stilled.

She held his gaze and her heart hardened. Not my business. A starving kid.

'I'll check,' he said at last, sounding goaded. 'I'll talk to Brenda.'

'When?'

'This concerns you why?'

'Because he would have sold his soul for a jam sandwich,' she said evenly. 'But even then... Do you know what he said when I packed the food for him? He said, "I can't take it home if Jack'll be hungry." He's been watching you. He thinks you're great.'

She watched his face freeze. Watched something working behind that grim facade. 'I don't want it,' he said. 'I've given them free rent. What else do I have to do?'

'Care?'

'I don't care,' he said explosively. 'If you want to stay on this farm, you need to get used to that. I keep myself to myself, and I expect you to do the same.'

'For six months?'

'Yes.'

'I won't let a kid go hungry.'

He raked his hair. 'Neither will I. Thank you for giving him the chicken.'

'There's no need to be sarcastic.'

'Believe it or not, I wasn't,' he said wearily, and went back to his sausages. 'I was thinking it's better that you help him than me. If anyone needs to.'

'Anyone does.'

'Right, then,' he snapped. 'Two sausages?'

She looked at the sausages. She thought of the delicate meal she'd had the night before. She felt her tummy rumble.

She'd had a very long day. She'd have an even bigger one tomorrow, she thought. Hard physical work. Horses. Figuring what was happening to Oliver.

Figuring how to make Jack Connor care.

'Three,' she said, and plopped down to watch her chauvinistic, arrogant, overbearing boss cook her dinner.

He tried to focus on cooking. Sausages needed only so much focusing.

Behind him, Alex was watching. He could feel tension rising. She was here for six months?

She'd have to learn the ground rules. He might have got himself an employee but he would not allow her to mess with his life. He was a loner and he intended to stay that way.

She was messing with his head.

As was Oliver. He thought back to the kid, eating Alex's sandwiches like he hadn't been fed for a week, and he felt ill. He didn't care, but...

'I'll go over in the morning,' he said, and Alex beamed.

'Can I come, too?'

'Sancha needs watching. As do the pregnant mares.'

'None of the mares in the home paddock look near to dropping, and it'll take us how long to visit Oliver?'

Us. The word hung.

'I have work for you,' he said roughly.

'I'm having a sickie tomorrow,' she said. 'On full pay.' She held up her blistered palm. 'Work injury. The boss is responsible. I read up on Aussie work laws before I came. They cover me nicely.'

'You're planning to sue already?'

'Nope,' she said, happily tackling her sausages. 'Just

go with you to see Oliver. He's a great kid. And I've been thinking... You could pay him to exercise Sancha for the next month. Just a little bit, but enough to help with food. He could take her for a gentle walk around the yard while the colt frolics. It'll save you a lot of time and he'd love it.'

'That's why I'm employing you.'

'You can employ me better working with the horses,' she retorted. 'Or even working on this house. Your veranda rail's about to collapse. Your window frames are rotten. If you get me some decent timber I'll rebuild.'

'You?'

She raised one eyebrow. 'Yeah,' she said. 'Um, maybe personal observations about my boss are out of line, but you do seem to have a time warp problem with the sexes. You seem okay with the cooking side, but the rest... If you'd employed a guy and he'd offered to fix your veranda, would you have an issue?'

'You're twenty-five years old and you come from Manhattan,' he said. 'You expect me to believe you can build?'

'I can strip most car engines, too,' she said, mock modestly. 'And I also drink beer. My daddy taught me right. Speaking of which...' She held up her glass of water with dislike.

He eyed her with disbelief. She eyed him right back.

He took a beer bottle from the fridge and handed it to her.

She raised one eyebrow, knocked the top off on the corner of the battered table and drank a quarter of the bottle without stopping.

He couldn't help himself. He grinned.

So did she.

'You sure your daddy wasn't right and you're a guy, after all?' he demanded, and she chuckled. It was a great sound, he thought. An amazing sound. It filled the old kitchen with a warmth it hadn't known for years.

It had never known.

Insidious.

He was not about to be sucked in by a woman's laughter. She was drinking beer. She was smiling.

They ate on and he thought…insidious.

He finished. Started clearing. 'Go to bed,' he growled. 'You'll still be jet-lagged. I'll fix the dishes after I've checked the horses.'

'Nope,' she said, and cleared her own things. '*We'll* fix the dishes after *we've* checked the horses.'

'There's no need.'

'I'm a vet,' she said. 'Sancha's my patient.'

'Suit yourself,' he said, more brusquely than he intended, but she beamed as if he'd said he wanted her to go with him.

Why would she beam if he said that?

It was too hard. He was way out of his comfort zone. He grabbed his hat and headed out into the night, leaving Alex to follow if she wanted.

It was nothing to him if she did or if she didn't.

Liar.

But it had to be nothing.

The night was warm and still. The horses were in their stall, totally at peace. Sancha looked up as he approached and gave a gentle whinny of recognition but she didn't move. She had her foal. All was right in her world.

At least he still had his horses.

He thought back to his shock when he'd arrived back here. When he realised how much Brian had been stealing.

His grandfather had hated Jack. When he'd taken Sophie away he'd told him he wanted nothing more to do with him, ever. Yet for all Jack's time in the city, the thought of the horses had stayed with him, vaguely comforting. In the awful times with Sophie, he'd known the horses were still here and the knowledge helped.

But they were only just here. Brian had been siphoning funds every way he knew how. After his grandfather died, when he hadn't left a will so Jack had inherited by default and started asking for accounts, Brian had told him he was paying for farmhands—but not. He'd told him he was maintaining the place but not. The only thing he had maintained was horse care. He'd still bred and sold the great Werarra stockhorses.

Maybe he knew if the horses had been maltreated Jack would come after him with a gun.

Melodramatic? Maybe not.

He thought of Brian and felt again the surge of the anger he'd felt as he drove unexpectedly through the gates and seen what was left of the farm.

He thought of Brian's wife the day Brian had fled. Another woman. A trail of fraud.

Brenda had been gutted. He'd done what he could to help, but...

But the judgement in Alex's eyes said it wasn't enough.

Brian's wife and family were none of his business. He was letting her stay in the house rent free. What else could he do?

But he'd been shocked seeing Oliver today. Why was he hungry?

And Alex's judgement...

Yeah, he'd have to go over there. Throw some more money at it. Make the problem disappear.

'Oliver is all ready to idolise you,' Alex said from behind him, and he stilled. He'd hoped she wouldn't follow. What was she doing, acting as his conscience? He did not need a chirpy vet from Manhattan telling him what to do. 'He's been watching you with the horses. He thinks you're great.'

'Oliver is nothing to do with me,' he snapped.

'I've heard Australia has a decent welfare system,' she said as if she hadn't heard him. 'I wonder what the problem is?'

'I'll fix it,' he said, far more savagely than he meant to. 'They can't stay here if she can't manage. I'll organise their transport back to the city.'

'That'll help. Get the problem off your patch.'

'I'm paying their rent. What else do I have to do?'

'I don't know,' she said evenly. 'Talk to them for a start. Find out what's going on.'

'I'll do that in the morning.'

'In your current mood you'll be offering removal vans.'

'This is not your business.'

'The kid's starving,' she said evenly. 'Of course it's my business.'

He raked his hair. She was right.

Was she going to be right for six months? A chirpy little conscience, telling him to get involved.

And it was working. He should have been involved, anyway. He knew Brenda was isolated. He knew she was a single mum with a husband who'd robbed her blind.

He knew she was needy.

He felt his fists clench. He did not need this. He did not need anyone to depend on him.

'We'll just go see,' Alex said cheerfully. 'You never know, it might be simple, like a broken-down car and she can't get to the shops. I can fix the car while you go shopping.'

'Alex…'

'If you didn't want me to get involved you should never

have left me alone with Oliver,' she said evenly. 'He's a great kid. The best. And he's desperate for help. I'm out there on a limb for him, whatever you do or don't do. Will we go over in the morning?' She met his gaze and held. 'It's Sunday. Day of rest. I can work if you like but it's time and a half, and time off in lieu during the rest of the week. Plus if I work when I've been wounded while working—'

'You've been reading—'

'My employment contract,' she said happily. 'It was a very long plane ride.' She grinned at him. 'Boss,' she said. *Boss.*

He'd sent her the standard employment contract he used for his IT company. It was meant for city workers. He hadn't thought this through.

She was employed for forty hours a week. For forty hours a week he had control. The rest of the time she'd be living with him but she was free to do what she liked.

Like interfere with his life.

He was being melodramatic again. She was wanting to check on a kid she'd met. Fine. She could come along for the ride. She could watch while he did whatever had to be done.

She'd want what was best for the kid.

So did he, he thought, as long as it didn't involve him.

Oliver's all ready to idolise you. He knew it. He could see the need.

He didn't want it.

He'd done enough caring to last a lifetime and it had achieved nothing.

'I'm going to bed,' Alex said, still watching his face. 'What time are we going tomorrow?'

'Ten,' he said, because there was no choice.

'Great.' She stooped and fondled the little foal. 'Okay, then, everything's settled. Wake me if you need me.'

'I won't need you.'

'I thought that was why you employed me,' she said softly. 'But have it your way.' Then she rose and smiled at him. 'Don't be grumpy,' she said. 'It doesn't suit you. Good night.'

And she was gone, closing the stable door behind her.

CHAPTER FIVE

SHE was up at dawn. He was out in the stables when he saw her leave the house. She was wearing jeans, T-shirt and riding boots. Her curls were caught back in a simple tie.

She whistled as she headed down to the creek and he felt an almost irresistible urge to join her. To walk along the creek and show her the property. To introduce her to the horses in the upper paddocks.

He didn't. He was cleaning out the stalls. Sancha was the first of a dozen mares due to foal in the next few weeks. He needed to get his nursery ready.

He'd have Alex here for the foaling.

The thought was both good and bad. To have a vet on hand was great. To have a chirpy blonde conscience was less than great.

He hoped she'd have a really long walk. He hoped she'd give him some space in the morning—but he was unaccountably peeved that she did.

She returned half an hour before they were due to leave for Brenda's, strolling up from the creek, looking windblown and flushed. She had grass seeds in her hair.

He came out of the stables and saw her crossing the yard and something inside him stilled. She was here, in his home.

She looked like she belonged.

She saw him. 'It's magic,' she called. 'It's utterly, wonderfully magic. I might even have stayed here if you hadn't
fixed the plumbing.'

'Liar.'

She grinned. 'Yeah, okay, maybe not. Oh, but, Jack, it's
fabulous. And the horses… I need you to introduce me.
I said good-morning to everyone, but it was really hard
when I didn't have names.'

'You'll learn soon enough,' he growled, thinking six
months… Six months when she looked like this…

'Did you get out of bed on the wrong side again?' she
demanded, and he winced. Was he so obvious?

'I'm always grumpy.' Why not say it like it is?

'Whoops,' she said cheerfully. 'But I'll ignore it. My
dad says my whistling in the morning drives him crazy, but
it's never stopped me. Can we ride over to Oliver's now?'

He'd like to see how she could ride. Her references said
she could, but then… 'I've saddled Cracker for you,' he
said, motioning to the two horses saddled and ready to go.

'Well, hi.' She approached both horses with just the
right amount of quiet and confidence. In a minute they
were her new best friends, with her rubbing just the right
spots of both horses at once. 'Don't tell me,' she said
cautiously. 'Your ride's the two-year-old with spirit and
Cracker's the rocking horse.'

She was good. A minute and she had them both summed
up. Maestro was his favourite mount, a spirited yearling
just broken. Cracker was getting on for twenty. He'd been
his grandfather's mount in his old age.

'No offence, Cracker,' she said, rubbing the old horse's
ear just where he most loved to be scratched. 'But your
owner's wanting to test my riding skill and he won't test
anything if I'm sitting on you.' She swung herself up into
Cracker's saddle with the skill of someone who'd spent

years on horseback. 'What say we take you for a ride up the back paddock before we go, and swap you for someone who needs a good, hard ride. Which is what I'm aching for. Or alternatively, Jack could ride you.'

'I won't have you risking your neck,' Jack growled.

'If you wanted a girl, you should have advertised for one,' she said evenly. 'I applied for a job as hand on a horse stud. You think I'd have done that if I didn't love horses?'

'Stockhorses are different from horses you'll have ridden.'

'Which is why I want to ride them,' she said evenly. 'Don't patronise me, Jack. Let me ride.'

They rode together to the top paddock where he kept the best of his stockhorses, those who were almost ready to sell. For many of his horses the initial training was done here, and Brian had managed to at least maintain that. They couldn't be trained to perfection—a decent stockhorse took years—but by the time they left they knew the rudiments of working with stock.

His grandfather had prided himself on never having a horse returned. Thankfully Brian's skills with horses had not been compromised by his dubious accounting practices so Werarra's reputation had kept going, and Jack had no intention of letting it slip.

Training took time, though, and energy, which was why the house was looking pretty much as it had when he'd walked back in. His horses came first.

They did for Alex, too. She rode Cracker a little way ahead of him and he watched her hands, her seat, the way her eyes covered the ground in front, searching for traps like rabbit holes. She tossed a few comments over her shoulder as she rode, seemingly relaxed, but he knew her horse was her first priority.

By the time they reached the top paddock he was almost looking forward to seeing her on a decent ride.

A decent stockhorse might dent her confidence, he thought, and uncharitably he thought it mightn't hurt that confidence to be dented. She was too...perky. She thought the world was a great place, that nice things happen to nice people, that life was fair.

He knew who her father was. Her people had serious money. This woman would have had everything she wanted, from birth.

Maybe it wouldn't hurt to challenge her with one of his decent colts. A colt with a bit of spirit?

Not a rocking horse. He felt himself grin.

'You planning on teaching me a lesson?' she threw over her shoulder.

What? How the...? How did she know what he was thinking? She was in front of him, looking away. She hadn't even seen his face.

She could read him.

The thought was so disconcerting he didn't know how to handle it.

'You asked for a stockhorse, I'll give you a stockhorse,' he said through gritted teeth, and she waved without looking back at him.

'Hooray. Thank you. Cracker, old boy, I'm sorry I won't be riding you. Let's have a bit of a gallop now. Are you up for it?'

And Cracker flattened his ears and showed he was.

She only had to ask, Jack thought grimly as he watched her fly across the paddock ahead of him. A Manhattan princess, she only had to ask and the world gave her what she wanted.

* * *

These were young horses and spirited. They were roaming free in the huge top paddock where the boundaries were so far apart you could stand in the middle and not see a fence. The country was wild and undulating. It was a magic place for a young horse to be, but catching them, bringing them in, would be a skill in itself.

Alex sat on Cracker while Jack headed down the paddock, holding back, letting his horse do the approaching, letting the young horses sense Jack was simply an extension of the horse he was on.

That's what he looked like.

Ellie and Matt, always the protective older siblings, had done a bit of research on this man before she'd come. Jack had left the farm when he was seventeen. He'd moved to the city, into IT. He'd created a company her brother told her was competitive on the world stage. He'd stepped aside as working head only a few months ago.

She'd hardly expected him to be here, or if he was, it'd be in an owner/supervisor role. She hadn't expected…this.

Wherever he'd been for the past few years, he hadn't lost his skill with horses. He was approaching the cluster of yearlings now, and the young horses were starting to edge away.

He moved almost before she knew his intentions, his horse speeding, turning, cutting off a young horse before it realised what was happening. Catching its bridle and reassuring it. Settling.

He made it look easy, she thought, stunned. He was leading the young horse back to her already. If it was Alex doing the fetching she'd still be galloping after it.

Did she have the skills for this job?

She didn't have the skills of this man.

He led the young horse to her, slipped off his horse and raised an eyebrow.

'You want to swap the saddle with you still on it?'

She felt like an idiot. She slipped from the saddle, and reached for the buckles.

Jack was before her. The saddle was clear, the blanket lifted across, the saddle set on her new mount—and she was just in the way.

'This is Rocky,' he said. 'Grandson of Cracker. He's frisky. You sure you can handle him?'

'I'm sure.'

He linked his hands but she shook her head. Rocky was big by stockhorse standards but she had no trouble swinging herself into the saddle.

And all at once she felt...different. Rocky was a fabulous mount, gleaming black, young and eager. This was a fabulous place, a fabulous day, her horse was gorgeous... and Jack was looking at her and smiling.

'You think you have his measure?'

'We'll see,' she said, thinking she had.

'Remember he doesn't know how to curve. He stops and spins. And you're not wearing a seatbelt. Take him for a canter round the paddock. Nice and slow. Beware rabbit holes.'

'Teach your grandmother to suck eggs,' she said, and grinned, and gathered the reins and touched Rocky's gleaming flanks. 'Let's go.'

Okay, she wasn't quite a Manhattan princess. He'd been gobsmacked with her veterinarian skills. Now, he watched her ride and she was simply an extension of Rocky. Girl and horse moved seamlessly together, as if they'd worked and trained together for years.

Rocky was young and willful. He'd expected it'd take her a while to settle him, but she had his measure from the get-go.

She walked him a little way, and he saw her speaking to the horse, bending so he'd hear, and he thought, *Horse whisperer.* This skill to communicate, to settle fractious horses, to make them feel like she was in control but it was pure pleasure to submit…

His grandfather had had it and it was the only thing he'd loved about the brutal old man. He'd thought he had it himself, but the years away from the farm had dulled his skills, his instincts. He'd get there again, he thought, but meanwhile…

Meanwhile he had this woman who could do anything she wanted with a horse.

Except.…

She'd allowed Rocky to move to a canter. She was heading along the long south boundary and he saw the moment she decided it was safe, she was in control, she could fly.

He hardly saw the moment she signalled to Rocky he could have his head, he could gallop as he'd been aching to gallop, but suddenly they were flying, girl and horse, and he didn't know which looked more wonderful.

Or maybe he did, but he wasn't going there.

They were nearing the eastern fence. Slow, he told her under his breath. Slow…

She didn't. Instead he saw her foot just touch Rocky's flank to guide him into the curve.

In most horses this signal was to curve, but to Rocky…

He didn't curve. He simply turned.

One moment Alex was as one with her horse. The next she was lying on the soft green pasture, staring up at the sky.

He'd warned her. He shouldn't have let her. He shouldn't…

He was with her in seconds, feeling ill. He'd known. If she was hurt…

She was lying flat on her back, looking straight up.

She looked awed and stunned. He slid from his horse and stooped—and she started to laugh.

Her laugh rang out over the valley, a low, gorgeous chuckle that turned his insides to water.

'Oh, my, you warned me,' she breathed. 'How stupid was that? Isn't he marvellous?' She held out a hand for him to pull her up, and she was still laughing.

He took her hand and tugged, feeling poleaxed. She came up fast, and she was right in front of him, her body touching his, her hand in his.

She looked up at him, and something caught within him, something he'd never felt. She was beautiful, pure and simple.

She was...

No. This wasn't just beauty. This was...

Danger. Step away.

But his hand still had hers and he couldn't let go.

'I'm guessing rein signal only for turns,' she said. 'Heels means stock work?'

'You got it.' He was having trouble getting his voice to work.

'Teach me.'

'Rocky will teach you.'

'His methods are painful.' She pulled back a little way then, but he saw something in her face, some acknowledgement that she was feeling the same sensations coursing through him. This tug...

He released her hand and it felt like a loss.

She glanced up at him, and then consciously turned away, watching Rocky rejoin his mates. She could have been hurt, he thought, but she was a horsewoman. The ground was soft after the rain. She knew how to fall.

'I need to double-check that contract,' she said. 'Am I

still covered for worker's insurance if I bust my butt on a Sunday?'

The tension eased. He grinned, and he thought, She's wonderful.

Do not go there.

To go down the path of caring...

What was he thinking? He wasn't thinking. It was a momentary aberration, a second's weakness and nothing more.

He swung himself up into the saddle and saw uncertainty, doubt, cross her face. Good. Only it shouldn't be uncertainty. It should be sureness that there would be no connection.

He was not interested in connection.

'I'll have to catch him all over again,' he said, more roughly than intended.

'Thank you,' she whispered, but he wasn't listening. He was turning to fetch her horse. He was moving on.

Oliver was sitting on the front step when they reached Brenda's. His bleached red hair was a bit too long, a bit too curly. His clothes were too small and his bare feet were filthy. His eyes lit up as he saw them, his beam almost splitting his freckled face, and Jack felt a surge of guilt.

Which was exactly what he didn't want to feel. He'd had enough guilt to last a lifetime. Sort this problem and move on.

'Is Brenda home?' he asked, and Alex shot him a look of surprise. Fair enough. It had been a curt question. Too curt.

'You want to hop up on Jack's horse while Jack talks to Brenda?' Alex asked, tossing him a look that might be interpreted as defiance. 'But only if you let me hold the reins.'

There was no hesitation. Oliver was down from the veranda before Jack was out of the saddle. Jack looked into his desperate little face, winced and lifted him high.

The kid swung into the saddle and beamed and beamed. 'I love Maestro,' he said simply.

How did the kid know Jack's horse?

'You're letting *her* ride Rocky?' Oliver demanded of him, and he could just as well have said: 'You're letting *a girl* ride a man's horse?'

'We've stuck some glue on her saddle,' Jack said, deciding it was impossible to be grumpy in the face of such pleasure. 'Do we need some on your saddle, too?'

'No,' Oliver said, mortally offended. 'I know how to ride. Don't I, Brenda?'

Jack turned and Brenda had emerged from the house. She was holding a toddler in her arms and a little girl clutched her leg.

She was wearing tattered jeans and a stained T-shirt. Her hair was long, in need of a wash. She looked almost emaciated. What the...

'I told Oliver not to go near your place,' she said in a dead voice. 'But thanks for the food. Oliver, get off.'

Something was seriously wrong.

He should have come here before this, he thought. He should have checked. Giving her a house rent free obviously wasn't enough. There was more going on.

And then, cutting into his thoughts came awareness of a car sliding into the clearing behind them. A large, black expensive saloon with tinted windows.

The horses startled back. He moved to check Maestro, but Alex had both horses firm and safe.

All the colour had washed from Oliver's face. Jack turned back to Brenda and found she looked the same.

Two guys emerged from the car. Cliché thugs, he thought. Like something out of the movies.

They should be wearing black suits and black ties and sunglasses. Instead they were in casual gear, jeans and T-shirts, but their clothes didn't disguise what they were. They looked like nightclub bouncers. Heavy, tattooed and menacing.

The driver looked from him to Alex. 'We're here on business,' he said almost pleasantly. 'You want to take the little lady for a ride while we talk to Brenda?' He smiled at the horses. 'Nice gee gees. Worth a quid, are they?'

'Two and six at the knackery,' Jack said, pseudo-pleasant, back. 'Brenda, would you like us to stay?'

'I...' Brenda looked from the men to Jack and back again, and her fear was obvious.

'We're staying,' Alex said. 'Brenda wants us here.'

'You going to sell a horse to help pay her debts?' The momentary niceness was slipping.

'What debts?' Jack asked.

'Brenda's hubby borrowed a whole lot of money,' the guy said, leaning back on the car and folding his arms. 'From my boss. My boss has been patient but the drips Brenda's been feeding us aren't enough. My boss loses money, he gets annoyed.'

'Brian stole money from me, too,' Jack said.

'Join the queue, then,' the guy said evenly. 'She pays us first.'

'Blood out of stone.' Jack's voice was carefully neutral. Impassive. Blunt. 'You think I'd have left anything if there was anything worth having? The bank's been in this week, declaring her bankrupt. They've gone through her assets like a dose of salts and now they've even put a garnish on her pension. She gets food for the kids at the local store and that's it. Every other service goes through the bank. Look at her... She's at rock bottom. No one's ever getting money here. Meanwhile Brian's sitting pretty on the Gold Coast. I can give you his address if you want.'

'Yeah?' The guy stared at Jack, alert. 'We can't find him.'

'His girlfriend's mother came whining to me last week,' Jack told him, watching Brenda, not him. 'The mum's just discovered her retirement savings have disappeared and there's not a lot of motherly love left. She thought a nice forwarding address might be useful to me. If you guys are interested...'

'We're interested,' the guy said.

'Excellent,' Jack said. He motioned to Brenda. 'I'm starting to feel sorry for her. Three kids... She's starving. I give you the address, you leave her be. Deal?'

'I dunno...'

'I'm not exactly without threats myself,' Jack said, and suddenly he wasn't Jack any more. He was, Alex thought, a guy who'd been raised as tough as these guys. 'I've half a dozen men employed on my place who know how to handle themselves.'

Whoa. He sounded mean and he looked mean. This was a don't-mess-with-me voice and the guys responded.

'No need to get your knickers in a twist, mate,' the guy said, suddenly placating. 'It seems reasonable. Though if it's a false address...'

'No promises but he was there last week.'

'Then we'd better get moving,' the guy said, and laboriously wrote the address on the back of his hand and signalled to his henchman to take off.

Leaving Brenda and Oliver and Alex, all staring at Jack.

'I hope you didn't want to protect the...' Jack started, and then looked at Oliver. 'The other party in the negotiations,' he corrected himself, and Brenda gave a sob that was simply heart-rending.

And Alex was off the horse in an instant, shoving the reins into Jack's hands, flying up the veranda steps and gathering the woman into her arms.

What was it with women? How did they do this?

Alex had never met Brenda in her life, and here she was hugging her. It made him feel…

He wasn't sure how it made him feel.

Yes, he did. It made him feel like an outsider, looking in.

That was what he wanted, wasn't it?

'Is Brenda crying because you made them go away?' Oliver asked, puzzled. 'She doesn't like them.'

'Have they been here often?'

'Every pension day,' he said. 'Only last pension the grocer said if we didn't give it all to him that was the last food we were getting and the men were really angry. They said they'd come back today. Only you made them go away.' He was high on Maestro, gazing down at him, and Jack could see hero worship, clear as day.

Uh-oh. He did not want this. A bereft kid who lived next door, who loved horses…

It was bad enough having Alex for six months. She'd been here for one day and already he could feel the outside world sucking him in.

Caring?

On the veranda Brenda was recovering. She turned to face him, within the safety of Alex's arms. Alex was holding her like a mother hen hovers over a chick.

This was not Alex's business. Had no one told her?

'You lied,' Brenda managed. 'You've never taken a cent from me. And you don't have half a dozen men on your farm.'

'If I'd come across as your defender, they would have been back. It seemed the best way.'

'But Brian's address?'

'That much is true. His girlfriend's mother was robbed, too, and she's vitriolic. She hoped I might do something with it. Today, seeing how he's left you, the least I could do was pass his address on to someone who cares.'

She gasped. 'Do you know how much he owes?' she demanded. 'And Brian's been living like royals.'

'I guess even royals have to face reality sometime,' he said. He glanced at Alex, who was watching him with a faint smile. She approved, he thought. She'd made him care? Yep, she'd sucked him right in, and she was pleased with herself.

'You guys need to go shopping,' she said happily. 'What if Jack and I take you tomorrow?'

Whoa.

He froze—and Brenda saw his expression and responded accordingly.

'I don't have money for shopping, and even if I did, I wouldn't trouble you further. You've done enough for us.'

'When's next pension day?' Alex demanded.

'Thursday week, but—'

'My family is wealthy,' Alex said, and she glanced at Jack and her glance told him exactly what she thought of him. She'd seen his expression. His lousiness was noted and she was moving on. 'It would be my real pleasure to take you shopping and buy you what you need to get you through to next pension day.'

'I won't take charity,' Brenda said in a strangled voice, and Jack knew that was all about his expression. She assumed he'd looked like that because he thought he was put-upon. When, in fact...

Yeah, okay, it was true; he did feel put-upon, but not financially.

He did not want to be sucked in.

'It's not charity, it's pleasure,' Alex was saying, stubbornly, glaring at him. 'And we don't need Jack. But he's my boss. If he'll give me time off…?'

It needed only that. He was the boss. She was asking permission to help someone he should have known was in trouble. She was asking permission to care for someone he should have cared for himself.

We don't need Jack.

He was being let off the hook. That was what he wanted. Wasn't it?

He glanced at Oliver. The boy's face was screwed in puzzlement as he tried to figure what was going on. He looked at Alex, who was carefully not looking at him.

He could sense her anger.

He'd protected Brenda from the debt collectors. He'd given her free rent.

Alex's expression said she'd expected more of him, and she was angry because he wasn't giving.

What right had she to be angry? No right at all.

They were all waiting for him to respond. To tell Alex she could have time off to give Brenda the help he should offer himself.

'No,' he said, and it was as if someone else was speaking, not the Jack he knew. 'Brenda has enough debts, she doesn't want more.'

'I'd never ask her to pay it back,' Alex said hotly, but Jack silenced her with a look.

'I'm offering Oliver a job,' he said, and he looked directly at Brenda. He was blocking Alex out, even though every nerve in his body was tuned to the judgement he saw there. 'One of my mare's just had a foal by caesarean section,' he told Brenda. 'She can't be allowed to run free, yet her foal needs freedom. Which means someone has to walk her gently for an hour at a time, for at least the next six weeks. Oliver, if you'll do that for me, twice a day at weekends and once a day on school days, I'll pay in advance by taking you all shopping tomorrow. I'll buy decent clothes. I'll cover your groceries until next pension day and I'll cover your fuel bills here. Is there anything else you need, Brenda?'

Brenda gasped—and so did Alex.

And from Maestro's back, Oliver's eyes grew enormous.

'I'm going to work to pay for our food?' he gasped.

'That's the one,' Jack said.

'By walking Sancha?'

'If you agree.'

'Yes,' Oliver said, so fast they all laughed.

Or the two women laughed. Jack watched them laugh and wondered just what he was letting himself in for.

Alex had been here for two days. Any longer…

Any longer, he didn't want to think about.

CHAPTER SIX

THEY returned to Werarra. Oliver arrived half an hour later, ready to take up his duties. Alex went with him to exercise the mare.

Jack headed back down the paddock to fix fences.

Sound carried a long way in the valley. He could hear them chatting like long-lost friends, and he thought, They're two kids.

Only they weren't. Alex was every inch a woman.

In years, he thought, but in truth she was still a child. She had no idea how much emotional entanglement hurt.

It didn't always. Other people had successful family lives.

Other people were lucky. Other people gambled because they didn't know the odds.

Like Alex didn't know the odds.

He wouldn't be the one to tell her.

He worked until dusk. When he finally reached the house he found a brief note on the kitchen table.

Jet lag. Head's still somewhere over Hawaii. Had an egg on toast and gone to bed.

He should have come up earlier, he thought, and then he thought no, this was good. This was back to normal.

Maybe they should have separate meals.

He ate alone. He always ate alone, but tonight it felt different.

Bleak.

He headed back out into the night to check the mares before he went to bed, and while he walked he thought he'd headed to this place for peace. He'd found it, but then along came one perky little vet from the U.S., pushing her nose into his business, messing with his equilibrium.

You've never had equilibrium, he thought.

It must be somewhere. He just had to find it.

Shopping with Brenda was fun—or it would be fun if Jack wasn't with them.

That wasn't exactly true, Alex thought, for from the time he'd loaded Brenda and the kids into his SUV, he'd set himself to be pleasant. He and Alex sat in the front. Brenda and the kids sat in the back. 'This feels like a family,' Oliver had said in deep satisfaction as they set off, and she'd seen Jack's mouth tighten and the mood for the day was set.

They arrived at the Wombat Siding shopping centre, a small plaza providing services for the surrounding farming community. Jack said something about farm tools and disappeared.

It was up to Alex to bully Brenda into trying clothes on the kids, steering her away from cheap and nasty, insisting she choose quality—and then Jack appeared at the end and settled the tab.

He did the same in the supermarket. Alex was having fun in the unfamiliar Australian environment—'What is this stuff called Vegemite?' and 'Do you really eat kangaroo?'—but she would have enjoyed herself more if Jack seemed more relaxed. It would have helped them all.

'Have you made him do this?' Brenda whispered at one stage, and that was the last straw. When Jack turned up at the checkout counter she turned on him.

'Brenda thinks this is charity,' she snapped at him. 'It's not. It's Oliver's wages. You know how much it'd cost you to have a trained vet nursemaid your horse every day, and you know Oliver's value. You need to get involved here, Jack Connor.'

'You can't speak to your boss like that,' Brenda whispered, appalled, and Alex grinned, unabashed.

'Why not? I just did. He's getting a good deal with me, too. I'm cheap for a vet and if he sacks me he'll be completely dependent on Oliver.' She was angry, but she tried to make this light. She managed a cheeky grin at her boss. 'Right. Brenda needs clothes for herself so this next bit is women's business. Jack, I need you to take care of the kids. There's a playground over there—'

'I don't do child care.' He looked horrified.

'Oliver will tell you what to do,' she said. She'd been carrying Brenda's rather grumpy two-year-old and she handed the baby over before he—or the toddler—could object. 'Here's Anna. Tracy, you go with Jack and Oliver and Anna. Jack will buy you all ice-creams. Your mum and I need some girls' time out.'

And she steered Brenda away before Jack knew what hit him.

He was sitting in the middle of a shopping plaza playground, surrounded by mums and kids. Oliver was whooping on the trapeze. Four-year-old Tracy was crawling through a worm-shaped tunnel. Two-year-old Anna was dripping ice-cream onto his knee.

He felt...he felt...

'Dadda,' Anna crowed, and it needed only that.

He looked at four-year-old Tracy and he saw Sophie. He looked at Oliver's gaunt young face and he saw Sophie.

He never wanted to feel like this.

One female vet who didn't know how to mind her own business…

'If I get on the swing, will you push me?' Tracy demanded.

'I need to hold Anna.'

'I will,' Oliver said, squaring his shoulders.

Oliver was having fun on the trapeze. There were a couple of boys his age, having a game with him.

He was climbing off the trapeze to do what Jack should do.

'I'll manage,' Jack said manfully, and heaved himself to his feet. Anna dropped her ice-cream and wailed.

'You need to multitask,' a broad grandma-type advised him kindly. 'You give me money and I'll buy the littly another ice-cream. The deal is that you keep an eye on my grandkid while I go.'

'Fine,' Jack said helplessly.

'Hey, it's fun if you just relax,' the grandma said. 'Lighten up and enjoy yourself.'

Alex and Brenda bought more in half an hour than Alex could believe. Clothes shopping in Manhattan was a serious business, but Brenda wanted it done fast. She was mortified that she needed help, but if she had to accept, then she was going to do it as quickly as possible.

Four pairs of jeans, T-shirts, windcheaters, a coat, smalls—Alex searched the shop, Brenda barely tolerated trying things on, Alex paid with the money Jack had left with her and they were done.

'I should never have agreed,' Brenda whispered as they

made their way back to the playground. 'I hate taking charity.'

'It's a lot harder to receive than to give,' Alex said, hugging her. 'Giving makes you feel great. So that's what you're doing. Making Jack feel great.'

'He isn't...'

But then they rounded the corner—and he was.

This was a different Jack. Both women stopped in their tracks and stared in amazement.

Jack was in the middle of a muddle of mums and kids and grandmas. An elderly grandma was sitting on the padded floor, holding Anna. Anna's face was practically buried in her ice-cream. The grandma was jiggling her and giggling, and the giggles were echoing around them.

There were two swings, side by side. Two little girls, Tracy and another who looked like she matched the Anna-holding grandma.

Jack was behind the swings. He was pushing, very carefully.

For out the front was Oliver, holding two ice-creams aloft. Ready for a lick a swing.

Jack's pushing had to be perfect.

If he pushed too little, the girls didn't reach their ice-creams. If he pushed too hard, the little girls' tongues would act as a bat and swipe the ice-cream out of Oliver's hands.

Oliver was holding the ice-creams for dear life. The little girls' concentration was absolute.

Half the population of the shopping centre seemed to have stopped, entranced.

Oliver was cheering, giggling, sneaking the odd lick of his sister's ice-cream, as well. He was turning into a kid again.

Alex found herself clutching Brenda and Brenda was clutching right back.

'See,' she said in a voice that wasn't quite steady. 'You've made Jack feel great.'

'You're great,' Brenda said, and her voice was just as wobbly. 'You've made this happen.'

'Nonsense,' Alex said, struggling to pull herself together. 'I didn't need to make anything happen. Some guys are a bit blind, but once they see… Jack's pretty great.'

'He is, isn't he,' Brenda breathed. 'And you're staying with him for six months?'

Her inference was obvious and Alex blushed.

''He's not that wonderful,' she retorted, and grinned. 'He hasn't bought us an ice-cream. You'd think a true hero would have all bases covered.'

Reluctant hero or not, he'd made Brenda happy. The little family sat in the back of the SUV and smiled and smiled all the way back to the farm.

But Jack looked rigidly ahead all the way, and Alex thought, Hmm, will he fire me the minute we leave Brenda's?

And then she remembered that two days ago she'd wanted to leave. Now the thought of leaving was appalling.

The parameters had changed.

Two days ago she'd been worried about leaving because she needed this job for her career. She didn't want her family thinking she'd failed. She didn't want to return to the States with her tail between her legs.

Now, she didn't want to leave because…

Of Brenda? Of Oliver?

Or because of Jack?

Because he'd looked wonderful pushing two kids on

swings. Because he'd made an entire shopping centre smile.

Because he'd made her smile.

That was a dumb thing to think. First rule for employment, don't fall for the boss.

She wasn't falling. How could she fall? But the transformation from a dark, shadowed enigma, to a guy who cared…

It was some transformation, and it was making something inside her twist.

'I don't like you staying out here by yourself,' he said to Brenda as they turned into Brenda's yard, and she thought, What? Is he about to offer to have them stay in the big house?

How many sausages would he need to cook, then?

'Would you like Alex to stay over tonight?' he asked, and she stilled.

She didn't say anything. She couldn't. He was her boss. He'd stipulated he'd provide accommodation. He hadn't specified where.

'I'm fine,' Brenda said. 'You need Alex at the farm in case the mares foal.'

Yes, you great lump, Alex thought, shooting Jack a private glare that could have frozen lesser men.

'Do you have parents?' Jack said, meeting her gaze fleetingly and moving on. Like this conversation wasn't about her.

'There's only my sister,' Brenda said.

'Would you like to go to her? Where is she?'

'I might,' Brenda said. 'But she's in Brisbane. It'd cost a fortune to move.'

'I might be able to help you.'

Here we go, Alex thought grimly. Pay to have the problem leave.

'No,' Oliver said, panicked. 'We can't leave the farm.'

'It was only your father who wanted the farm,' Brenda retorted. 'But you're right, we can't leave yet. Oliver has to pay back our debt.'

Oliver subsided but still looked anxious and Alex jumped right in. As was her wont.

'You can't move. We love having you here. And we love Oliver helping with the horses.' Alex was beaming back at Oliver, trying to make things better, but suddenly things had changed.

Jack's face grew grim.

'Don't we, Jack,' she prodded, knowing she was going too far but unable to help herself.

'Of course,' he said stiffly, and even managed a smile.

Oliver settled, happy again, but Alex knew, she just knew, she was in serious trouble.

They arrived at Brenda's, unloaded Brenda, the kids and their stuff, then headed back to Werarra.

With just her in the car Jack was back to looking grim.

She should ignore it, she thought. But then, when had Alex ever kept her peace? She'd spent her childhood in a conflicted family. She'd spent her childhood trying to make things right and she wasn't stopping now.

'What's wrong?' she said at last as the car drew to a halt.

'Leave it, Alex,' Jack snapped. 'You've had your way.'

'My way as in helping Brenda?'

'Yes.'

'So you'd have done nothing?' She took a deep breath, feeling a familiar surge of anger. It was the anger she felt when her father was unfair to his oldest two children, ignoring Matt, saying something cutting to Ellie. It was the helplessness she'd learned in a childhood when her father obviously didn't do what was just. But right now that anger, that helplessness, was directed straight at Jack.

'Oh, that's right. You *did* nothing,' she snapped. 'You did nothing until I poked you into reluctant action. How long has Brenda been coping on her own? She's your neighbour. I might live in Manhattan but even we know what's happening with the people in the next apartment.'

'Okay, so I should have checked,' he said, slamming the door of the SUV with a force that could have taken it off its hinges. 'I agree. Satisfied?'

'You'll keep checking?' she demanded, climbing out of the car after him, coming round to his side and keeping right on prodding.

'It seems I don't need to. My conscience will do it for me. I thought I was employing a farmhand with veterinarian qualifications. Not someone who's demanding I take the weight of the world—'

'Brenda's hardly the weight of the world.'

'She's not. And neither's Oliver or the two little girls, but as of today they're dependent.'

'So what?'

Enough, she thought, but she was still fuelled with anger. There was no way she was staying here for six months if Jack Connor was a boorish, uncaring oaf.

But the thing was, she knew he wasn't. He'd been wonderful today.

And now she was pushing him to stay being wonderful.

She could see conflict written all over his face. This wasn't coldness, the lack of passion of someone who truly didn't care. He looked...on the edge of a chasm, she thought, and the edge was crumbling.

'My big brother and sister did some research on you,' she said, softening a little, backing up a little. Her anger had flared but in the face of this man's confusion it ebbed to nothing. 'Matt was especially worried about me coming to the middle of nowhere to work for a guy he knew nothing about. So he had you checked. He says you built an incredibly successful IT company from nothing. He says your staff thinks the world of you, though you always hold yourself apart. Matt likes that—he said it's important not to blur employee/employer lines. But I'm wondering if it's just employer/employee lines. Is it everyone?'

He didn't answer. Well, why should he? He looked impassive, she thought, like what she was saying was nothing to do with him.

She should shut up now—but when had she ever?

'He also said your sister overdosed a few months ago,' she whispered. 'Rumour has it that Sophie had major problems all her life. Matt says talk within the company had you caring for her for ever. So I'm thinking, this was your grandfather's farm. There's been no talk of parents. Matt couldn't find anything out in the time he had, so I'm guessing, for all intents and purposes, there weren't any. I'm seeing one guy caring for his sister and losing, then deciding not to care again. Am I right, Jack?'

And the look on his face...

She'd gone far too far. She'd stepped right over the employer/employee boundary, and she'd kept right on going.

His face was like thunder. He was staring at her like she was something that had crawled out of a piece of cheese.

Apologise, she thought. But then she thought no, an apology would achieve nothing. She'd said it. Why not stand by it and face the consequences?

What did she have to lose?

Her job?

Maybe, but she thought of Oliver...

'If you cared, you could make Oliver's life good again,' she told him.

'No.'

'Because of your sister?'

'Alex, if you can't keep out of my personal affairs, then leave. Your choice.'

'I'm not good at minding my own business.'

'Learn.'

She glared but he gazed back, impervious.

What now? He'd been good to Brenda today, she reminded herself. He'd asked Oliver to work here. Maybe things would happen without her pushing.

But why did it seem that there was something wonderful right before her, something just out of reach…?

She was being fanciful and she was being dumb. She was putting her job on the line when Jack had already done what she'd asked.

Step back.

But she'd hurt him. She looked into his face and saw exposure.

She'd been right about his sister.

Before she could stop herself she reached out and took his hand.

'Jack, I'm sorry,' she whispered. 'Yes, I was out of line. Yes, your relationship with your sister is nothing to do with me, only I'm seeing someone who's trying to be a loner but not succeeding. You can't be a loner and react to those kids like you did today. You like people. You care.'

He stared down at her, looking baffled. He gazed at their linked hands like he didn't know what they were doing. Like this whole conversation was beyond him.

'I don't care,' he said roughly, as though it was a mantra. 'You come here, you come on my terms. You were supposed to be the guy who comes in and helps with the heavy work, helping me get the place back to where I can run it by myself again. If you can't accept the rules, then leave. I can cope on my own.'

'You'll always need a vet.'

'I can get one from town at need.'

'You'll lose horses.'

'It's the price I need to pay. When I get this place back to what it should be, I can set up accommodation, get decent staff, have it running like it should be running.'

'And step back again?'

'I won't need to step back. The place will run itself. I can stay living here—'

'In isolation?'

'So what's wrong with that?'

'Nothing,' she said stubbornly. 'If you were a different kind of person. But today I saw you with those kids and I know you're not built to be a hermit.'

'And you're not paid to be a psychoanalyst.'

He was still holding her hands.

And she was still holding his. There was a difference—but he hadn't pulled away.

Maybe he hadn't noticed, she thought, but there was no not noticing in her camp. She was noticing like anything.

'I'm not a shrink,' she managed. 'But I am a vet. I can recognise pain when I see it.'

'Then go and look at the horses. Do what you're paid for. Look for pain there.'

'I'll do that,' she said, but she still didn't let go his hands.

'Alex?'

'Mmm.'

'Don't do this.'

'What?' But she knew very well what he was talking about. She was gazing up at him, her eyes not leaving his, her hands still holding.

She could see him warring with himself.

He wanted her?

Was she crazy? If he did want her, she should run a mile.
She didn't run. She held him.
She waited.

It was four in the afternoon. There were horses to be fed
and watered. He needed to ride up to the back paddocks
and check the mares.

He shouldn't be standing beside his car, staring down
at a pert, blonde American with a penchant for sticking
her nose where it wasn't wanted.

He wanted nothing to do with this woman. She was
a mistake. She was a woman when he'd wanted a man.
She was smiles, laughter, caring, when he wanted none
of those things.

He should pull away now. He should turn his back on
her and go care for his horses, who asked nothing of him.

She was waiting for him to pull away.

The problem with pulling away was that he wouldn't
get to kiss her.

Whoa.

Kiss her? Now there was a crazy thought. This woman
was his employee. It was the middle of a Monday afternoon and there was work to be done. He needed a working
relationship with this woman, boss to employee, formal,
distant, workmanlike.

But she was looking up at him and she was worrying
about him and it was doing his head in.

No one worried about him. No one had to.

'Jack…'

And the way she said his name… It twisted something
inside him that had no right to be twisted. He hadn't been
aware it was possible to feel like this.

Exposed? Fearful?

No. What he was feeling wasn't fear. It was something

far deeper, and far, far sweeter. It was as if life had thrown him a constant barrage of sour lemons, yet here was something sweet and wondrous, something he hadn't known existed.

She was gazing up at him with concern, and her concern was doing his head in. Or more. It was the fact that she smiled; she made Oliver smile. It was the way she drank beer like a guy and then grinned at him. It was her skill with horses, the way she heaved wood, her unexpected strength.

It was the way she was looking at him. It was the way the sun was glinting on her burnished curls.

Her eyes were wide, watchful, and her hands still held his.

'Jack…' she said again and what was a man to do?

That one word did his head in. That one word dispelled all caution.

Sensible or not, he did what he had to do.

He bent his head and he kissed her.

Alexander Patterson had been kissed before. Of course she had. She was cute and blonde and her family was part of Manhattan's Who's Who. She'd been regarded as a desirable girlfriend for as long as she could remember, and she'd enjoyed being a girlfriend.

She'd had some pretty cute boyfriends. None serious. She didn't do serious. But she did do kissing, or she'd thought she did.

But this wasn't kissing as it existed in the past world of Alexander Patterson. This was something else.

What was it with this guy? He had something…

Something indescribable.

From the moment his mouth touched hers, the warmth and the heat of him, the strength, the sheer masculinity of this man, seared straight into her body, and she felt herself begin to burn.

He hadn't wanted to kiss her. She'd known it. And okay, it hadn't actually been all his idea. She knew how to get a guy to kiss her and she'd looked up at him and held his hands and she'd wanted it.

If he was a terrible kisser she had only herself to blame, but nothing was further from the truth. She felt her lips fuse to his, she felt a weird buzzing sensation in her head, she felt her arms wrap round his broad, strong body and she felt... Or maybe she shouldn't feel. Maybe she should just be.

There didn't seem much choice. He was plundering her mouth, demanding response. He'd taken her face between his hands, tender yet firm, centring her, holding her, and the intense sensation was enough to make her weep.

She felt beautiful, desired, beloved?

Beloved? Stupid word.

Maybe she'd asked for this kiss. If it worked, it was a way to make the guy know he was human. Kissing was a game she was good at. It was nothing more.

But this...this was everything more. This was...

Jack.

Oh, the feel of him. The taste of him. The pure, raw strength of the man she held.

She clung and kissed and let herself be kissed and she felt herself change, transform, turn from a silly kid trying to make this guy human to a woman who wanted this man so much that if he swept her up right now she'd—

'No.' The word was wrung from him like it caused sheer physical pain to say it. Those same lovely, tender hands were putting her away from him with a strength she didn't believe possible, and she could have wept.

'N...no?'

But no it was. He was holding her at arm's length, and he was looking at her as if she was an alien from outer space. Like she was nothing he recognised.

'I don't want this.' The words seemed to be wrung out of him.

'I didn't think I did either,' she whispered, touching her mouth, which felt swollen and bruised. And hot. Really hot. 'Maybe, maybe I was wrong.'

'We have to live together for six months,' he growled. 'That's not going to happen if we can't keep our hands off each other.'

'I don't know,' she managed, trying to make her voice casual. Trying to find the strength to make a joke out of what was anything but humorous. 'That'd mean we only had to renovate the one bedroom.'

His breath hissed in. He stared at her like she'd grown two heads. He definitely thought she was alien, she thought. A scarlet alien.

'I do not want—'

'Of course you don't,' she said, and she was proud of the way she made her voice sound almost polite. Almost indifferent. 'And neither do I. But I'm a practical girl and did you know my bedroom roof leaks? But of course, a day on the roof and a bucket of nails is far less complicated than sharing your bedroom. So, shall we get on with our evening chores? You check the back paddocks, I'll see to Sancha. By the way, you need to decide whether you want to replace the red gum wood used to build your veranda posts or go for something cheaper like treated pine. So much to think about… Oh, and I bought Chinese takeaway for dinner. All we need to do is reheat it. Hooray, no sausages. Now, any other instructions…boss?'

How had she done that? A part of her was inordinately proud of herself. Somehow she'd made it sound like that kiss meant nothing. She'd made it sound like she kissed guys all the time, and this had been just one more kiss.

She'd made it sound like it didn't matter, but she looked into his face and she knew that it mattered a lot. And for her... She knew it mattered more than anything she'd ever felt in her life.

'Don't fall for the boss.' She heard her brother's advice ringing in her head and she thought, Too late, too late.

How could she have fallen in a matter of days?

She hadn't, she told herself savagely. This must be jet lag, loneliness, pure emotional nonsense. She was moving on and he was, too.

'Right,' he said in a voice she didn't recognise. 'Horses first.'

'Horses, it is,' she said, and she made herself sound cheerful. She made herself grin. 'Let's get on with it.'

'I shouldn't have—'

'And neither should I,' she said. 'It was the way you handled Anna. There is nothing sexier than a man with a baby. Remember it and stay clear in future. It's a wonder you weren't jumped by every woman in Wombat Siding. So enough of the kissing, and let's get on with what we need to do. Six months' work, coming up.'

CHAPTER SEVEN

FROM that moment on, Jack's new veterinarian and handyman threw herself into her work like it was the only thing in the world that mattered.

Alex worked with the speed of a guy, and the skill of two men.

She left him stunned.

The kiss was forgotten. Or maybe it wasn't completely forgotten. It was like the kiss had created new boundaries. They knew what would happen if they approached those boundaries and both of them were steering clear.

Alex had relaxed, though. The kiss seemed to have cleared the air, allowing her to be who she was. She worked with cheerfulness as well as skill. She whistled, she strolled the paddocks as if she belonged; she loved the horses, and she revelled in the beauty of his property.

She teased him, she laughed at him, she demanded he teach her how to handle a stockhorse…and every time he turned aloof she put her hands on her hips and glared.

'You want me to kiss you *again*?'

She was treating the kiss as a joke?

But it was the right thing to do, he conceded, as the days turned to weeks. The kiss had happened. If they skirted round it, it'd stand between them, a barrier to any normal relationship. By laughing about it, they could forge ahead.

And they were...forging.

When he'd employed Alex he'd hoped to get some decent farm help. That Alex was filling that function was doing his head in, but he had no choice but to accept it as fact.

He was almost totally occupied rebuilding neglected fencing. Maybe if she'd been a guy, maybe if the kiss hadn't happened, he'd have her helping, but he wasn't going there. He didn't intend spending every day working alongside her. He'd decided if she spent her time caring for the horses, making sure his pregnant mares were okay, she'd earn her money, but that was never going to be enough for this woman.

She made lists and demanded timber. She rebuilt the veranda rail and he couldn't believe the job she did. She repaired window frames.

She would have repaired the roof but he drew the line there. The ancient slates were slippery and brittle. He wasn't game to touch them himself, but in the face of Alex's determination to have a non-leaking roof he employed a roofing company.

'Wow,' Alex said two weeks after arrival. She was cooking her specialty—pasta—which seemed pretty much the only meal she knew how to cook. 'A working bathroom. A roof that doesn't drip. A veranda I can sit on—what luxury. If you're not careful you might have me for ever.'

'If you learned to cook I might want you,' he growled, and she grinned and passed over a loaded plate.

'Real men don't eat pasta?'

'Not every night.'

'Every second night,' she corrected him. 'Interspersed by your turn. And your sausages aren't so hot.'

'I do a neat poached egg. Aren't girls supposed to like cooking?'

'Only if they don't like hammering nails. My mom told me if I want to get on in life, I should never learn to cook and I should never learn to type.'

'Your dad and mom sound great.'

'They are,' she said. 'Mostly.'

'And sometimes not?' He hadn't meant to ask. They didn't cross personal boundaries. The question just seemed to have come out all by itself.

'Sometimes not,' she said, humour fading.

'Want to tell me about it?'

She gazed across the table, astonished. As if she'd never expected such a personal question. Fair enough. But it wouldn't hurt to relax a little, he thought. After two weeks, those boundaries were solidly in place.

'There are four kids in our family,' she told him. 'Ellie and Matt are twins—they're the oldest. Then there's Charlotte and finally me. We ought to be one big happy family but my dad's always played favourites. There's nothing he won't do for Charlotte and me, but for Ellie and Matt…it's like he always does what's fair. It's like he's pretending to love them and it doesn't work. He and Matt have been at each other's throats from the time I can first remember, and Ellie… Dad snaps at her and she stops eating. She's been struggling with anorexia all her life. It's made for a stressful home life—but not as stressful as yours. What were your parents like?'

He'd walked right into that. You tell me yours, I'll tell you mine. Could he now say, Mind your own business, and refuse to reply?

'My mum was single and flighty,' he told her, deciding to stick to facts. 'When Grandma was alive it was okay but after she died, things fell apart. Mum took off when I was eight and Sophie was six. Grandpa disappeared into grief and the bottle, and from then on we fended for ourselves.'

'You were left caring for Sophie?'

'Yes,' he snapped, and wished he hadn't.

'Ouch,' she whispered. 'And then she got sick. That makes our family fights pale into nothing.'

'We survived,' he said, but then he thought, No, *we* hadn't. Sophie had crumpled.

And she saw it. He looked across the table and he saw recognition of his pain.

He did not want this woman feeling sorry for him.

'So no one taught you to make anything but sausages,' she said thoughtfully, and he realised with relief that she wasn't following through. Maybe she realised how much he didn't want to go there.

'A bit of invalid cookery, too.' That was as far as he was prepared to go, and she saw the flicker of recognition for what lay behind those words.

'Maybe we could learn,' she said thoughtfully, and he thought, What?

'Sorry?'

'If I'm here for six months… At home we have a gorgeous maid who cooks like a gem. What if I write to her and ask to send us her favourite recipes. If I make one every second night, and you do the same, we could have fun.'

Fun. Fun was so far from where he was at, he felt flummoxed.

She was suggesting they use this big old kitchen for what it was meant for—cooking. Real cooking.

He thought back to the distant memories of when his grandmother was alive—a kitchen full of warmth and the smell of baking, and of kindness. It was a faint echo, insidious in its sweetness.

Don't go there.

But Alex was looking at him like an expectant puppy, big-eyed and eager.

'You do it,' he growled.

'Not if you don't, too,' she retorted. 'Don't cook or type. That's my mantra—unless I'm working for a guy who's prepared to cook and type, as well.'

'You reckon these fingers can still cope with a keyboard?' He held up a broad, work-worn hand and she grinned.

'Maybe not, so we both give typing a miss. But I'm thinking you don't need skinny fingers to make a peach pie.'

'Peach pie?'

'Maria's favourite.'

He gazed at her across the table and she gazed back, chin tilted, challenging.

Cook. In this kitchen. With this woman?

Nope. Not with this woman. He'd be cooking every second night while she did evening stables. And vice versa.

Fun?

Her challenging gaze said it could be fun. Eating Alex's peach pie.

Maybe he could hurry his turn at evening stables and watch her cook. A bit.

And in return?

Not peach pie. His gaze wandered to the shelf beside the stove, to a mass of cookery books. To one in particular, an ancient school exercise book, crammed with cutout recipes and handwritten notes.

His grandmother had died when he was seven, but before then that recipe book was out on this table every day.

Alex was following his gaze. 'Your grandma?' she asked, and he nodded.

'So Maria will be teaching me and your grandma can teach you.'

What was it about those simple words?

They made it feel like the kitchen could come alive again. Like it could breathe. He felt the echoes of the warmth he'd felt when his grandmother had lived, and he looked across the table at Alex and saw...

He wasn't sure what he saw. There was nothing of his grandmother in Alex. No shadows of the past.

But a promise of the future?

Ridiculous.

'Deal, then?' Alex asked, and he nodded, curtly.

'If you want.'

'You want, too,' she said.

Did he? No. He was doing it to humour her. She was right, sausages and poached eggs and pasta weren't a balanced diet. Her suggestion was sensible.

'I'll see if she has recipes for steak as well as sausages,' he said, and she grinned.

'You'll have to do better than that, boss,' she said. 'This is a competition. Every night we rate our dinner out of ten. At the end of six months, the winner gets to pay for a degustation meal in Sydney's best restaurant as a farewell dinner for me.'

'I can't leave the farm,' he said, startled. 'No.'

'You can't run the farm without help,' she said evenly. 'You know that. You need to get training solidly under way for the colts in the top paddock. You have a great breeding program going and that takes time, too. There'll always be disasters needing your attention. And how are you going to attend the sales, get to market, do what you have to do? I'm one of a long line of employees, Jack Connor.' She gave a cheeky smile. 'I may well be your best but I won't be your last. So my replacement will take care of the farm while you and I have a first and last date. Degustation meal in Sydney the night I leave. Deal?'

'Deal,' he said because he couldn't think of anything else to say.

They'd kissed, he thought, and then they'd moved on. Now she was proposing they could have one dinner together in Sydney, as she left. And that'd be the end of it.

'Excellent,' Alex said, and beamed. 'I'm off to email Maria. And you need to start reading. Winner gets to choose the restaurant. I'm starting research now.'

They'd achieved a deal with cooking. They hadn't achieved a deal with Oliver. Alex had taken him on as her personal project, and she was like a pesky battering ram with her demands for the child. Her demands weren't big enough to knock him over but they were bothersome all the same.

The kid came over after school, twice at weekends. He took Sancha out into the home paddock and gently led her round, let her graze and kept her controlled while her foal frolicked around her.

That was fine by Jack. It was what he'd agreed to. He even liked that it gave the kid pleasure. He was all for giving the kid some pleasure but what he didn't like was the way Oliver looked at him. Like he was some sort of superhero.

Sophie had looked at him like that. No matter how bad life got, she had an infallible belief that Jack could fix it.

There was no way he was going down that road again, no matter how hard Alex pushed. He knew, too well, that encouraging dependence did nothing, achieved nothing, and only meant future pain. When Oliver arrived he normally headed down to the creek, found fencing projects far away when the kid was here.

But Alex pestered him to stay, and finally, stuck in a stall waiting for a mare to foal, she fronted him directly.

'What is it with you and Oliver?' she demanded. 'He's aching to help more. You let him walk one horse. What he'd really like to do is ride. There are quiet mounts. He already loves Cracker. Why can't we let him?'

'I don't want him getting attached to this place.'

'He already is attached,' Alex retorted. 'You know he's had a rough deal. Brenda's not his mum—she's his step-mum. She's kind to him but it's not like he's her own and he knows it. His dad's disappeared. His mum's occupied with his two half-sisters. Thanks to you he has enough to eat and he's safe but he needs more.'

'If Brenda needs more help—'

'Brenda doesn't need more help,' she said, exasperated. 'But she's talking of moving back to the city to be with her sister. It's breaking Oliver's heart.'

'Kids are tough,' he said, thinking they have to be.

'When your mum walked out on you,' she said thought-fully. 'Did the horses help?'

'This is not about me.'

'It's not,' she said evenly. 'It's about a little boy who needs your help. Are you afraid he'll depend on you like Sophie?'

Whoa. How had she got there? She was supposed to be a vet, not a shrink.

'This is nothing to do with you, and you need to be careful yourself. You'll return to the States. If you build a relationship, where will he be then?'

'With you.'

'You just said his mother's taking him to the city.'

'She's not his mother.'

'All the more reason not to get involved, then,' he

snapped. 'He needs to build a relationship with her. You're not suggesting I should adopt the kid, let him live here?'

'No, but—'

'Then it's kinder to put boundaries in place now.'

Silence.

They were sitting quietly at the rear of the stables, waiting for the mare to drop her foal. Maybe Alex had thought this was a good time to bring up Oliver, he thought grimly—when he was distracted enough to agree.

He wasn't agreeing to anything. Especially not to a freckle-faced, needy kid who could just as easily self-destruct.

He hadn't been able to make a blind bit of difference with Sophie. What did Alex think he could achieve with anyone else?

The mare gave one last, mighty contraction and the foal slithered out onto the hay. Unlike Sancha's, this was a fast, trouble-free birth. Alex checked the tiny muzzle, made sure there were no breathing problems and stepped back. The least human intervention while they bonded, the better.

Job done, they slipped out of the stall and stood looking down at mare and foal across the stable door. One tiny, gangly foal, learning his new act of balancing on legs that looked crazily inadequate, his mother, gently nuzzling, helping her baby find his feet.

It never ceased to feel amazing, Jack thought. He loved this part of the job, and having Alex here took the tension away, knowing he had a vet on hand.

He had her for another five months. After that he'd find decent help. Men who respected his boundaries.

Instead of one slip of a girl who worked like two men.

Who tried to shove one waif of a kid into his care.

'Is she okay?' The wavering voice came from behind

them. Oliver. Or course it was Oliver, here to take Sancha for her evening walk. But he was asking the question of Alex. He cast Jack just the one, nervous glance. Respectful. Hopeful.

Scared.

The thought made Jack feel a bit ill, but there was nothing he could do about it.

He knew he'd only make things worse.

'Alex can introduce you to our new foal,' he said brusquely. 'I have work to do.'

'A long way away,' Alex said dryly.

He didn't bother to answer. He left them to it, woman and child admiring one new foal.

He walked away, down to the area he was fencing, which just happened to be at the far boundary of the property.

She had no right to ask him for any more favours, he told himself. Oliver was fine.

But Brenda wasn't his mother. He'd seen the kid's expression when he'd gone to see her in the days after Brian left. The boy had seemed terrified as well as bereft.

Terrified he'd be alone?

He wasn't alone. He had Brenda. And he had Alex, who was putting her heart where it wasn't wanted.

Only it might be wanted. With Oliver?

She was going back to the States.

Steer clear, he told himself. Stick to your horses, and don't care.

He couldn't care. Caring was the way of nightmares.

Oliver walked Sancha and then Alex drove him home. He'd walk, but this way he could spend more time with Sancha, more time on the farm he so obviously loved.

He was always quiet on the way home, his small face growing stoic.

His stoicism was doing something to Alex's insides.

When she was a teenager her dad had taken her with him on a business trip to South-East Asia. She'd loved the experience, the food, the culture, but she'd been appalled at the poverty.

On her last day there she'd found a dog. It was half-grown, starved, pathetic. She'd fed it satay sticks from a hawker stall and demanded her father organise to take it home.

'We can't do that,' he'd said gently, citing disease, quarantine, so many problems for an animal that was half-dead. 'Don't feed it any more, Alex. You're prolonging the agony.'

She hadn't been able to walk away. She'd moved heaven and earth but she still hadn't been able to bring him home. Finally she'd insisted they find a veterinary clinic and have him put down.

And Oliver?

She couldn't take him home either. Oliver wasn't starving.

But he was starved of affection. She'd seen Brenda's sparse greeting as he returned home—'You're late, your dinner's in the oven'—and she'd thought, Push Jack some more?

He was already pushed to the limit. He was relaxing in her company. They were enjoying their cooking competitions. He was almost having fun.

'I have five more months,' she said out loud. 'Maybe by then I'll make him relax enough to fight for Oliver.'

But if Oliver reminded him of Sophie…?

'I should be a shrink,' she told herself. 'But then, I'm not so sure a shrink could get past those barriers either.'

She pulled to a halt in front of Werarra, taking a moment to admire her handiwork, the steady new veranda rails, the patched and painted window frames. Jack had cleared the weeds from along the front and remnants of an ancient garden were creeping through again. The place was beginning to look as it should.

Five more months… Too little time.

'You shouldn't be thinking that,' she told herself. 'You should be missing your family.'

She headed into the kitchen where Jack was attempting chicken cacciatore. It smelled fabulous.

He was wearing an apron. His grandmother's. A flowery apron over jeans and T-shirt.

It should look ridiculous.

It looked so sexy it made her toes curl.

He pointed to the mantelpiece. 'Mail,' he said.

That distracted her. Mail. Real mail? Not email. Who'd be sending her a real letter?

She picked it up and felt a weird sense of foreboding. It was a crisp, linen-weave envelope, old-fashioned. The kind of paper she knew her sister Ellie had a passion for.

Ellie's writing.

Ellie emailed her when she needed to communicate, so what was this letter about?

'This won't be done for fifteen minutes,' Jack said grimly. 'Or more. I seem to have a heap more cacciatore than chicken. Unless you want soup, you have time to read your letter in private.'

And then he glanced at her face, and his brows snapped down in concern. Maybe he saw her apprehension.

'I'll read it on the veranda,' she said.

'Take your time.' Jack met her gaze for a long moment and then returned deliberately to his casserole. Giving her space. 'It's thin soup at that.'

CHAPTER EIGHT

SHE didn't come in after a quarter of an hour. The casserole was less soupy—almost edible.

After half an hour the casserole was perfect but she still didn't appear.

He removed his apron, set the casserole to the side of the stove and went to find her.

She hadn't gone far. She was sitting on the edge of the veranda, holding her letter in her hand, staring sightlessly across the paddocks to the mountains beyond.

She looked shocked and defeated.

He sat down beside her without saying a word. Just sat.

'If it's really bad news people telephone,' he said gently. 'Usually. But this...what's so bad that it can only be told by snail mail?'

'My family,' she whispered, and he waited.

He knew so little about her, he thought as he waited. Her father had Alzheimer's. That was an appalling disease, but she'd known about it before she left. What was this?

'Your mum?' he asked.

She didn't say anything.

'You want me to bring your casserole out here?' he asked gently. He wouldn't push. Heaven knew he was the last to invade someone's privacy.

But he wanted to. The look on her face... He couldn't bear it.

'Or would you like to talk about it?' he heard himself say.

There was a long, long silence. The dusk was falling, the last hint of crimson sunset fading behind the distant mountains. The smell of his grandmother's roses, freed at last from their matt of weeds, pervaded the warm evening air. A flock of cockatoos was settling to roost in the massive gums behind the house, their squabbling for position making a weird evening symphony.

If this was bad news there were worse places to receive it, he thought. Worse places to come to terms with what was in her hand.

Would she tell him?

Did it matter?

But suddenly it did.

Maybe it was a Dear John letter. Did she have a boyfriend back home? He'd assumed not. The kiss...

She'd returned his kiss with a passion that said she was heart-whole. The look on her face now said she was anything but.

'It's ancient history,' she said into the stillness. 'It's nothing. But it's everything.'

She stopped and he thought, Don't push. She needed time.

He went inside and served two helpings of his casserole, carrying them outside. Maybe he should eat inside and let her be, but something about her face had him not wanting to leave her alone; had him believing his presence might even help.

If she'd had to receive bad news, he was suddenly absurdly glad that she was here, in this place. This night.

The stillness. The sound of the cockatoos. This farm had become his solace. It had its own form of healing.

She lay her letter aside and ate her casserole. The news can't have been too appalling, he thought. She was still hungry.

She cleared her plate and managed a smile. 'Eight,' she decreed.

'Eight?' he demanded, mock offended. 'That was a ten worth of effort.'

'The chicken's a bit stewed,' she said. 'It's shredded. Maria cooks cacciatore. I don't think it's supposed to be boiled for hours.'

'That was deliberate,' he said. 'You look upset and distracted. I was being considerate. I didn't want you choking while chewing.'

She smiled, but absently.

Ask.

Why?

He didn't seem to have a choice. The look on her face...

He was involved, like it or not.

'Would it help to tell me why you're looking upset and distracted?' he said gently, wondering at himself. He didn't get involved in employees' lives. He didn't care.

Right now, though, he found himself caring a lot.

But she didn't answer.

He carried the plates inside. Washed up. Thought about leaving her to it.

He couldn't. He walked back outside and sat and watched the moon rise over the valley.

He sat on the far side of the veranda steps to her. He was giving her space, but still he stayed.

A man and a woman...waiting?

'There was always something wrong in my family,' she said at last, and it was as if the words were a sigh. A long, drawn-out acceptance of sadness. 'There was always something. This…' She lifted the letter and waved it blindly towards him. 'It's from my sister. It explains so much.' She took a ragged breath and then corrected herself. 'But maybe…maybe she's not my sister,' she added. 'My…half-sister?'

'You want to explain?'

She stared down at the letter. It was too dark now to read it—he hadn't turned on the veranda lights and he didn't intend to. The moonlight created the illusion of privacy, a space where maybe she could talk. For a moment he thought she wouldn't, but then she sighed again and rose and stared out over the valley.

'My mother married twice,' she said. 'Fenella—my mom—had what she described as a disastrous first marriage and she found peace and security with my dad. My dad's great. He adores me. He adores my sister, Charlotte. But the twins… Ellie and Matt are older than us and he should love them to bits, but instead…he's kind, like Brenda's kind to Oliver. Like he does the best he can but it's not real. And now I know why.'

'You said half-sister.'

'It seems my mom was pregnant when she married.' She gave a half laugh. 'Actually we knew that—Ellie discovered birth and marriage certificates long ago. We've teased Mom about it, and she always laughed and said she and Dad were blindsided—couldn't keep their hands off each other. But now, what Ellie's found out… It seems Mom was pregnant from her first marriage. Mom lied. Matt and Ellie aren't Dad's kids at all.'

Silence.

'I guess…that happens,' he said at last, softly, cautiously, and she nodded.

'No big deal?'

'I can imagine it's a huge deal for your family, and especially for the twins.'

'I'm not sure how they'll react,' she said. 'Knowing there was a reason my dad didn't care.'

'But it sounds like he did care.'

'No,' she said strongly, almost violently. 'Caring's when you give your heart. Dad never did that for the twins. He did all the right things, like Brenda's doing for Oliver. Like you're doing for Oliver. You're doing what you need to do, what Oliver needs for survival, but you're not giving your heart. You know, when I think back to all those years, to Dad calling us Charlie and Alex rather than Charlotte and Alexandra, making it clear he was aching for a boy because he didn't want Matt to succeed him—being nice to Ellie but not playing with her, not hugging her like he did Charlie and me... It breaks my heart and now I know why. I want to go home and punch him. How could he have taken the twins in when he didn't have room in his heart for them? And now he has Alzheimer's and I still love him to bits, but the hurt he's given Matt and Ellie... What a lie for them to carry. And you know what? Their real father's dead. After all this time, they can't do anything. My mom and dad robbed them.'

He didn't move.

There were accusations against him in all this, he thought. The way he was treating Oliver...

That was hardly fair.

But this wasn't about him, though. It was about Alex.

'But you know what?' she asked, sniffing almost defiantly. 'In all this, Ellie's written to say she's fallen in love. She's met the man of her dreams and he sounds awesome. He's some sheriff in Larkville, Texas, where her real dad came from. So she's happy. That leaves only Matt...' She sniffed again.

'You love your brother.'

'Like you loved Sophie, I bet,' she said. 'Even if he's only my half-brother.'

'Use the house phone if you want to call him.'

'I will.' She sighed. 'In a while. Not now. I need to get my voice in order first.'

'You want to go for a walk along the creek?'

'It's too rough,' she said, sounding surprised.

'There's a track on the far side. I have a decent flashlight. We might even spot a platypus, and I promise to keep you safe from drop bears.'

'Drop bears?'

'Weird Australian marsupial,' he said. 'They cling high in the branches and drop at the first sign of life below. You're walking along and thump, there's a drop bear covering your head. Their claws are so long they usually need surgical removal. It's quite a business, carting drop bear victims to hospital with drop bear attached. It'd be easier to shoot the drop bear but they're heavily protected. If it's a choice between an American vet or an Aussie drop bear, the drop bear wins every time.'

She stared at him, her mouth open. And then slowly, the strain on her face disappeared and was replaced with a grin.

'You're joshing me.'

'Why, yes,' he said, grinning right back. 'Yes, I am.'

She giggled, and it felt good. More, it felt great. To take the strain from her eyes...

To someone with practically no family—okay, no family at all—it was hard for Jack to get his head around Alex being appalled to find two of her siblings had different fathers. He was pretty sure he and Sophie had different fathers, but he'd never bothered to ask or find out. It simply wasn't important.

With Alex, though, there was a goodly part of her that was a protected child of a wealthy American family. Up until now her world was black and white. Parents didn't lie. People were supposed to care. She couldn't see that caring had its own consequences, its own costs.

He thought about her family from her dad's point of view. The twins weren't his. Maybe he'd thought one day their real dad would make a claim. He may well have only been protecting himself.

Like Jack was doing with Oliver?

Like he was doing with Alex.

'I'm carrying the flashlight,' Alex said. 'Plus I'm wearing a hat. I might not believe in drop bears but I do believe you have pythons.'

'That'll hug you to death in seconds,' he said in a voice of dire warning.

'Just lucky I'm not huggable,' she retorted. 'And I know exactly what your nonvenomous pythons can and can't do. With hat and flashlight I'm fine. If you show me where to go I could go by myself.'

'Huggable or not, you need an escort,' Jack said, and then added, almost to himself, 'I care at least that much.'

They walked silently through the bushland, along the rippling creek, through country that looked weirdly different at night.

If Jack hadn't accompanied her she wouldn't have ventured far, she thought. Not that she was afraid of phantom drop bears and pythons, but it was dark and there were rustlings in the undergrowth and the moon wasn't bright enough to show the way.

But Jack had suggested it.

And Jack was with her.

She was shining her flashlight on the path ahead. Jack

was walking behind and close. Like a big cat, he didn't need a flashlight.

She was suddenly absurdly aware of an urge to drop back, to take his hand and let him lead her through the night.

Which was crazy. She didn't want him to.

Did she?

She shouldn't. This guy was her boss, a solitary farmer with so many shadows in his past he'd never get through them.

But tonight he'd cared. He'd fed her his casserole and he'd listened to her story.

He could have told her she was being dumb, that having two siblings who were now only half-siblings was no big deal. But he hadn't mocked her. Instead he'd stood back with eyes that were warm with sympathy and understanding, and he was here now, aware that she couldn't simply go to bed after news like this, that she needed to walk it out, to take time to come to terms with it, to take in the night.

The path was growing nearer to the creek. A line of rocks ran across as a mini-ford and suddenly Jack was grasping her hand, tugging her back.

'Wait,' he said softly, and he dug into his pocket and unfolded paper. Another pocket produced tape.

Cellophane. Red. 'What the…?'

'My grandma showed me this trick just before she died,' he told her. 'Grandpa was away at the horse sales and she brought Sophie and me down here.'

He fastened the cellophane over the flashlight. Instead of a piercing yellow beam, they now had a diffuse red glow.

'You need to be quiet,' he said softly. 'Look right into the middle of the creek, where the rocks form protection for the tiny night feeders.'

He held the flashlight and he took her hand in his again, leading her out onto the rocks.

The rocks were steady. There was no need for him to hold her but he wasn't letting her go.

And she didn't pull away. She couldn't. This night... the sound of the rippling creek...Jack—the combination was doing something to her insides.

The aching pain of an hour ago was fading to unimportant. There was only here, only now, only where Jack was taking her.

He led her right into the middle of the stream, then squatted on his haunches, tugging her down with him.

'Watch,' he whispered, and directed the flashlight into the water.

She looked and saw crystal-clear water running over smooth pebbles. The light was attracting insects, tiny moths and bugs.

There were traces of weed in the water. She watched on and saw the flash of silver, fish, no bigger than her thumbnail.

The more she looked, the more she saw. A whole universe was beneath the flashlight.

'Wait,' Jack breathed, and she waited, silent as the night, content to do what Jack told her, content to let this moment take however long Jack decreed it should take.

'This is the best place,' Jack whispered. 'If we're patient...'

And then he paused.

A platypus.

By the light of the flashlight she could see it clearly. It was little more than twelve inches long, covered with streamlined fur. What looked like a duck's bill was an elongated snout covered with soft, leathery skin. Its webbed feet looked weirdly incongruous.

It swam with its eyes closed, sensing its food rather than seeing, sweeping a yabby from the rocky bottom, snaffling a fish, almost surfacing to catch one of the moths that had fallen from the glow of Jack's light.

She'd seen one once, in a zoo, but here, seeing this wild, weird creature in its own habitat, the sensation was indescribable.

She couldn't believe she was here, in this place. With this man. Unconsciously—or almost unconsciously—her hand slipped back into Jack's and held.

She needed his hand to steady her. Or maybe…maybe she just needed his hand.

'He's a hungry little guy,' Jack said, seemingly unaware of her hand in his, but holding her with a warmth that was doing something to her insides. 'He needs to eat at least a third of his body weight every day.'

'I wonder if he likes chicken cacciatore?' she managed, and he grinned.

'Nicely stewed. Should I ask?'

'That's my breakfast you're offering,' she retorted, and went back to watching.

The little creature seemed oblivious to their presence. Maybe he thought the flashlight was the moon. Maybe he didn't see it at all. For whatever reason he grazed on, surfacing every now and then, heading to the bank to digest what he'd found, then returning to the hunt.

Her legs were beginning to cramp but she didn't want it to end.

'If we stay here much longer we'll need to call for a crane,' Jack said at last. 'My legs are going to sleep. Mind, yours are a lot younger than mine. You want to stand and tug me up?'

She grinned and did, and he stood too fast, and he was too close.

Or not close enough.

The night closed around them. The stillness turned to intimacy. The intimacy to need.

But yet...

'I don't want to hurt you,' Jack said into the silence, and her world stilled.

'How could you hurt me?'

'I don't do...close.'

'Then you'd better move away,' she managed. 'For we seem to be very close.'

'I should.'

'I guess...so should I.'

Neither moved.

She wanted, more than anything she'd ever wanted, to take his face in her hands, to draw him to her and to kiss him. But he was still and silent. His face was grim, and she thought, There's a war going on in here.

She'd taken one kiss. She'd been given one kiss. She'd made light of it, but if she went any further...

If she kissed him now, she'd end up in his bed. She knew that with the last shards of common sense that seemed left to her.

Was that what she wanted?

Maybe it was, she conceded—but she wanted more.

This was more than physical, but he didn't want it to be more. He had scars she had no hope of healing, hurts she had no hope of reaching.

If she let him take her to his bed, it'd make things worse. She was here for five months. This job was important to her.

If what was between her and her boss exploded, then she'd be gone and what hope then?

What hope of reaching him if she risked that?

Her thoughts were tumbling crazily through her head

as she looked up at him, as he gazed down at her in the moonlight, as the platypus continued grazing in the water at their feet.

He wanted her. She could see it in his eyes. His entire body was stiff with wanting.

But he was holding back. Knowing that to kiss her…

'Can I tell Oliver he can ride a horse tomorrow?' she said, and her voice came out crooked, desperate. Not how she wanted to sound at all.

Why had she asked that?

Because he needed to care, she thought. If he didn't care…

All or nothing? Start with Oliver.

'No.' He moved back from her, almost imperceptibly, but she noticed.

'Why not?'

'Because the boy needs a father,' he said, so harshly that she faltered and the creature in the water beneath their feet slipped silently into the darkness and disappeared. He glanced down and winced. 'See what you've done? It may not eat again tonight now that I've frightened it.'

'You've frightened me, too,' she retorted.

'You're not frightened. You're pushy.'

'Yes,' she conceded. 'You should be getting used to it.'

'Believe it or not, I am,' he said grimly. 'But I'm not about to let you talk me into something that'd be so disastrous.'

'What's disastrous about letting Oliver ride?'

'How could I not let him continue riding when you go home?'

'Would you need to?'

'Yes,' he said, and raked his hair. 'Yes, I would. Of course I would. Hell, Alex—'

'It's not,' she said, working on staying calm. 'It's not hell at all. It's giving one little boy pleasure by letting him ride.'

'You and I know it's more than that,' he snapped. 'You said yourself, Brenda's not his real mother and she's not acting like it. He's desperate for real parenting. When his father finally comes to his senses—'

'Is that likely to happen?'

'It has to happen.'

'He never talks about his dad. He talks about you.'

'And how's that supposed to make me feel?'

'Wanted.'

'I do not wish to be wanted.' It was almost an explosion. 'I wish to be left alone. I don't want a kid hanging on my heels. I don't want a kid worrying about me, missing me if I go to Sydney to the sales, always needing me. I don't want to be worrying about him.'

'And there's the crux of it,' Alex said shortly. 'That's what my dad never did with the twins. He never once let them close enough to worry about them. He did what he had to do.' She hesitated. 'Okay. The twins were short-changed but maybe something's better than nothing. Maybe you could let Oliver care for Cracker and take him home. He could ride at his place. You could pay Brenda for the feed and care. Hope Brenda does the worrying.'

'You don't leave a kid alone with a stockhorse, old or not,' he snapped.

'So buy him another.' She took a deep breath. 'A safe, kid mount. I'll buy him another, only it'll have to seem like it comes from you.'

'Why?'

'Because Oliver doesn't care about me,' she said, through gritted teeth. 'If you knew the pleasure it'd give Oliver to have you hand him a horse, keep an eye on him, teach him as he ought to be taught...'

'I do not want that kind of commitment.'

'Coward,' she said, and stepped from the rocks and slipped and ended up knee-deep in the stream.

She didn't swear. She simply stood with the clear creek water rippling around her legs, cooling her as she needed to be cooled.

Jack held out a hand to help her out. She ignored it. She glared at him and stepped back onto the rocks and squelched to the bank. 'I'm going home,' she said, grabbing the flashlight and ripping off the cellophane. Platypus watching was over. He could stay in the dark, alone. 'Don't come with me. I need to vent spleen.'

'Don't get lost.'

'What would you care if I did?' she snapped. 'What would you care if everyone got lost?'

He didn't follow her. Instead he stayed where he was, not moving, not thinking, simply trying to quiet his mind.

In a while the platypus came back. So much for his accusation that it'd stop feeding tonight. It wasn't afraid. Without the flashlight he couldn't see into the water but he could see it when it surfaced, to breathe, to digest the food it had gathered in its pouch.

A solitary creature.

Or not. This might be a female, desperate to eat to store fat and burrow to breed.

'Don't do it,' he told it—or her—and winced at his own stupidity. The world had to breed.

People had to care—just not him.

But he did care, he thought, growing angry. He'd sorted Brenda's problems. He'd allowed Oliver to help. The kid was now safe and fed, with a woman who'd do the right thing by him. Until his father came back.

And if his father didn't return?

The thought was bleak.

It was nothing to do with him.

Alex's fierce prodding made it everything to do with him.

Alex had to butt out. Alex was nothing to do with him either.

He must not care.

CHAPTER NINE

How to keep a working relationship after a night like that? He'd thought he couldn't, but Alex rose the next morning determinedly busy, demanding to see medical records of each individual horse, deciding they needed a more pro-active method of vaccinations, planning a database that would include every detail of every horse from planned conception on.

When it rained she worked on her database. When it was fine she worked outside, either hands-on with the horses or on her woodwork projects.

She was pleasant to him. She asked for orders and tried to sound deferential. She smiled when he smiled. They did the dumb scoring thing at each meal but the pleasure had gone out of it.

The boundaries had been set. It was for the best, but he didn't have to like it.

He wanted it to end, and yet he didn't.

Oliver still came over after school and walked Sancha.

Alex always chatted to the kid but Jack stayed clear. He heard them laughing, he called himself an idiot for not joining them, but years of training, years of solitude, couldn't and wouldn't be erased.

And then of course came the day Alex decreed Sancha was recovered enough to be let free.

'She'll stay in the home paddock for a couple more weeks,' she told Jack. 'But there's no need for Oliver to walk her any more.' She hesitated. 'It'll break his heart.'

'You don't break your heart after a month of walking a mare,' he snapped. A month of caring? It took far longer than that.

'The horses are important to him.'

'Let him keep on walking her, then,' he said roughly, and she shook her head.

'Sancha's restive now and Oliver's no fool. I'll tell him tonight. It's a shame we haven't any other recuperating mares to keep him on. Mind, he tells me he's ridden horses since he was a toddler. You could use him to exercise—'

'No!'

'Fine, then,' she said stiffly. 'I'll tell him. Did anyone ever tell you you're mean?'

'I tell myself,' he said grimly. 'And it doesn't change a thing.'

She told Oliver that night. He meant to stay away but he just sort of happened to be on the veranda. He watched the kid's shoulders slump. He watched Alex's shoulders slump.

The kid walked away, looking like the world had crashed down around him. He reached the home paddock gate and turned and yelled.

'I will get a horse. I will, I will. Someone will let me!'

He closed his eyes, Oliver's pain searing within, as tight in his chest as it must be in the child's.

Why not give in to it?

Maybe caring wasn't a choice. Maybe it was already there, like it or not.

Dear God, he didn't want it.

The choice staring at him was invidious. Have nothing

more to do with him. Trust Brenda to take care of her own kid, or trust Brian to come back and claim him.

That path seemed mean and small. It *was* mean and small.

The alternative?

You couldn't just give yourself a little bit, he thought savagely. He'd heard the despair. He'd seen the aching emptiness in Oliver's eyes.

But he'd tried to fill it for Sophie and he'd failed. To try again…

What cost if he failed again? Unthinkable.

Alex wandered back to the house and stared at him with judgement. 'Well?' she said. 'Satisfied?'

'Don't.'

And suddenly she softened.

'It's tearing you in two, isn't it?'

'Nothing's tearing me in two.'

'You want to help but you can't.'

'If I want psychological assessment, I won't go to a vet.'

'I'm a human first, Jack. Talking might help.'

'Nothing helps,' he said savagely. 'Things were fine before you came.'

'You want me to leave?'

'Yes!' And then he hauled himself together. This was irrational. All he had to do was get his emotions under control, get his head back together and put things back on an employer/employee basis.

'No,' he corrected himself. 'Of course I don't. You're a fine vet and a great worker. I can even lean on the veranda rail without falling off.'

'I aim to please,' she said, striving for lightness, but it didn't come out lightly at all.

'You aim to get your own way,' he growled, but he managed a smile at the end of it.

'I do,' she admitted. 'I worry myself sick over Oliver.'

'If it's any consolation so do I,' he told her. 'I'll keep an eye on the kid when you're gone.'

'From a distance. That's big of you.'

'Doing it any other way will make it worse. He needs to forge a bond with Brenda. If I step in, then she doesn't need to.'

'That's an excuse.'

He closed his eyes.

'Okay, I'm sorry,' she said hurriedly. 'I know there's more to this than what I'm seeing. I'll shut up.'

'Are you capable of shutting up?' he demanded, and she looked up at him and a glimmer of a twinkle started behind her eyes.

'Maybe not,' she admitted. 'Ask my family. They treat me as an annoying little buzz fly—no matter how they swat me, I'll always zoom right back into their faces. But they love me regardless. 'Cause I'm cute. And I get things done. Like now. One of the mares in the top paddock was looking a bit lame this morning. I couldn't see anything wrong—I suspect she stood on a stone and bruised herself but she needs checking again tonight. I'll walk up there now.'

'I'll walk with you,' he found himself saying, and she shot him a surprised look.

'I'll buzz,' she warned.

'I don't mind your buzzing.'

'Do you promise not to swat?'

'No.'

She grinned. 'Okay,' she said. 'I'm used to dodging. I'll buzz and you'll swat. An employee/employer relationship made in heaven. What's more, you can carry my gear in case I need to do anything. Perfect.'

* * *

They walked up through the paddocks. The sun was sinking in the west, the night was warm and still, and they stayed silent.

Contrary to her promise she didn't buzz at all.

She worried.

Letting things be was not Alex's style. All her life she'd tried to fix the conflict between Matt and Ellie and her father. She'd never succeeded.

She wasn't succeeding now. If anything Jack was growing more aloof.

It was his right, she thought, trying very hard to be fair. No matter how much Oliver needed a male figure in his life, she couldn't force it, and the look on Jack's face when she tried... She was starting to think she'd do more harm than good.

So now she shut up and walked beside him and tried to concentrate on the small sounds of the night, the birds coming in to roost, the frogs in the swamplands by the creek, the crickets complaining that their heat was fading. It didn't work. She was totally focused on this man beside her. On his pain.

For pain it was. For the first time tonight, she'd clearly seen his refusal to help Oliver for what it was. It wasn't selfishness but an aching certainty that help from him would achieve nothing.

She could badger him for ever about the moral imperative of helping, but to intrude on that pain?

She didn't know all the facts, like she hadn't known the facts about her father and Matt and Ellie. The world was a complicated place. It took figuring out.

Her sister's letter had thrown her, made her unsure of her foundations, and in the face of that uncertainty she knew she had to back off from pushing this guy beside her.

'You haven't talked for five minutes,' he said at last. 'Are you ill?'

She smiled, absurdly relieved at his note of teasing.

'Nope. Just enjoying this night. I grew up with a little-girl adulation of anything horsey. My parents sent me on summer camps—to ranches where I could ride my heart out. Matt—my brother—often came, too. I'm not sure that he liked horses as I did but he liked getting away from the friction between himself and Dad. But we used to ride. Because he was older the owners trusted him to take care of me. For a kid who lived in Manhattan it was the best of times, just my horse and my big brother. Only of course there were always other kids, always camp leaders watching. Out here, for the first time in my life I feel free and it feels fantastic. I wish I could bring Matt out here and let him feel it.'

'Invite him for a visit.'

'He's too busy now, growing his own company,' she said. 'I wish I knew how they're feeling—both the twins.'

'Phone them.'

'Be a buzz fly?'

'Maybe they like buzz flies,' he growled. 'They have their uses.'

She grinned and to her own astonishment she found herself slipping her hand into his. She felt him freeze—and then she felt him deliberately, consciously relax.

Had this guy ever walked in the moonlight holding a woman's hand?

He was her employer. She had no business asking.

No, she didn't, but his solitude caught her as nothing had caught her before. She held, not tightly, but still she held.

They walked on and the silence deepened.

'I'm not…good at this,' Jack said at last.

'Holding hands with a woman? Didn't you have movie theatres when you were thirteen?'

'There aren't a lot of movie theatres out here.'

'That's an awful lot of catching up you need to do, then,' she said lightly, and swung his hand and chuckled—and then stilled.

As did Jack.

The sound came from behind them, above. A horse, being ridden down the slopes from the upper paddocks, towards the creek.

Slow at first, and then faster...

A horse sounds different ridden to galloping free. The nuances are different—weight, the struggle between control and freedom.

Definitely ridden. Really fast.

Oliver's yell sounded through her head as clearly as if he was yelling it now. *'I will get a horse...!'*

'It's one of the colts,' Jack said in a voice that sounded strangled. 'Oliver? Oh, my God, if he tries to jump the creek...'

And he started to run.

They didn't see what happened. It took them what seemed half an hour but in probability it was only three or four minutes. Jack was well ahead by the time Alex burst through the clearing to the creek's banks.

When Alex reached the creek, the horse, a young, chestnut gelding, was pacing, wild-eyed and frantic, riderless, no saddle, reins hanging free.

Jack was in the water, fighting the current, waist-deep, eyes everywhere.

It didn't take skill to know what had happened. Oliver had simply decided to take the horse home. He'd set him at the creek, but the horse had balked and done a one-eighty turn these horses were famous for.

Oliver must be in the water.

There was debris everywhere. It had rained over the past few days and logs and leaf litter were being swept down.

Jack was searching with frenzy born of desperation, hauling logs aside, moving with a desperation that looked almost like madness.

She was in there with him, searching herself, not thinking of anything but one small boy, one tousled-headed kid who had to be here. Who must be.

The hills here were steep, and where Oliver had tried to jump was near a bend. There was always a mass of logs here, caught, gradually working their way free to where the creek widened as it turned.

Water was washing against a dam of logs.

Jack's flashlight was sweeping the water, searching, searching...

A flash of...something.

The flashlight was dropped as Jack dived.

In the light of the dropping flashlight—a glimpse of red-blond curls, tumbling under the water...

Alex dived forward but Jack was before her. Right under the water. Then rising, holding, dragging a limp child from under a matt of wood and leaf and water.

Totally limp.

No!

But then, as Jack lifted him higher than his chest, higher than the mass of litter-strewn water, he stirred and whimpered and coughed—and then was violently, distressingly and wonderfully ill.

Jack staggered to the bank. He knelt, turned Oliver sideways to clear his airway.

Alex staggered to reach them, hauled off her T-shirt,

using it to wipe his face clear, to make him safe, to let him breathe.

Jack simply knelt, holding the boy in his arms while she tended to him. Alex darted one glance at him and that was enough. His face was devoid of colour, ashen, grim as death.

He held and held, while she cleaned Oliver and whispered to him that he was safe and Jack had him and he was fine, and she noted that Jack's hold tightened rather than loosened, as if he was coming to terms with how close they'd come to tragedy.

'Drummer...' Oliver whispered, his first word, dragged out of him as if his throat was still half-choked, and Jack closed his eyes as if the word had physically stung.

'The horse is fine,' he said, sounding strangled. 'It wanted only that. You nearly kill yourself and your first thought is for your horse.'

'I didn't want to hurt him.' The little boy's voice was a sob. 'I wanted Cracker but he was too far away, and to-night I just wanted a horse. I just wanted...something.'

It was a cry from the heart, a piercing sob that shook the night. That shook Alex to the core.

There was a long, long silence where they all practiced breathing.

'Well, he's not the horse for you,' Jack said at last, and she knew he was striving desperately for control. 'Drummer's hardly broken. He needs solid training before he's a safe ride.'

'I can...I can ride!'

'If you got reins on Drummer and got him this far then I see that you can,' Jack said. 'But you and he both need work. If you need a horse that much, okay, in the morning we'll talk about you taking and caring for Cracker. You can help me train Drummer. You can improve your riding skills yourself and we'll go from there.'

'You mean…?' Oliver could hardly speak. He was still limp with shock and fear, and yet in the moonlight there was no disguising the look of blazing hope. 'You'll let me ride?'

'If the choice is between that and killing yourself, I have no choice,' Jack said grimly. 'Now let's get you home, young man. Your mother will be frantic.'

'She's not my mother,' Oliver said in a voice that came close to breaking Alex's heart. 'She's Brenda and she won't even know I'm gone.'

'She will soon,' Jack said grimly. 'Maybe after tonight both Brenda and I need to do a rethink about what one kid needs.'

Jack took Oliver home. Alex caught Drummer, led him to the home paddock and the stables beyond, calmed him, groomed him and checked him for damage.

She could see why Oliver had chosen him. He was, quite simply, magnificent.

'It wasn't your fault,' she told him as she rubbed him. 'You have the skills to be a great stockhorse and Oliver has the skills to be a great stockman. But you both need training. Jack's your intermediary. I'm thinking it'll work for you all.'

She rubbed him longer than she needed, waiting for the sound of the SUV returning. Finally it did. She waited longer, for Jack to appear in the stables. He came in looking grim-faced, stressed to the limit.

'Is he okay?' he demanded, tight and gruff.

The horse. Of course he'd be worried about Drummer.

'He's fine,' she said. 'And quiet. I'm thinking he's figured he had a hand in something ghastly.'

'Not that ghastly,' Jack said grimly. 'And it wasn't Drummer's fault. He's never been asked to jump water before, so of course he did a U-turn.' He looked grey, she thought. Grey and sick.

'I'm so glad it turned out okay,' she whispered.

'Thank God we were there,' he managed. 'It seems sometimes, that not caring—'

'Hey, it wasn't your fault,' she said, giving Drummer a final stroke and opening the stable door to let him into the safety of the home paddock. 'You did what you thought was right. You forbade him to ride.'

'His father taught him to love horses,' Jack said. 'I knew not letting him ride was cruel.'

'And now you've fixed it.'

'I've talked to Brenda,' he admitted. 'She's so taken up with her own two girls and her financial mess that she hasn't seen Oliver's needs.'

'And now she has?'

'I don't know if that's possible. But he's coming here tomorrow. He can take full care of Cracker, even help me train.'

'Wow,' Alex whispered. 'Oh, Jack, that's wonderful.'

'Yeah, and you'll go home and I'll still be doing it,' he said roughly. 'If it wasn't for you, Alex—'

'This is none of my doing,' she said roundly. 'It's your call.' But she looked into his face and saw such a depth of anguish there that her heart twisted in pain. He'd been railroaded. He had no choice now but to care about this little boy.

And if he could care about a child…

Don't go there, she told herself quickly. She had five more months of employment. That was all. Then she had to move on.

Which was what she wanted—wasn't it? To return to

the States with glowing references, get herself a job with one of the big horse ranchers, to prove to her family and her friends that she wasn't just a cute blonde bimbo who'd trained to treat kittens.

That *was* what she wanted. Wasn't it?

It had to be. But this gorgeous, wounded hero standing right in front of her was changing something inside of her.

She wanted to take two steps forward right now, wrap her hands around his waist and hold him. And hold him and hold him, until the armour he'd so carefully built around himself disintegrated to nothing.

She took one part of one step forward—and he backed out of the stall and turned away.

'I'm heading up the hill. I need to make sure Oliver didn't leave any gates open,' he said, more roughly than necessary.

'Do you want company?'

'No,' he snapped. 'Go to bed.'

'Is that an order, boss?'

'If that's what it takes,' he said grimly. 'Good night, Alex.'

'Good night,' she whispered, rebuffed.

'Oh, and, Alex?'

'Yes?'

'Thank you for today,' he said. 'We got him out and we kept him alive. I'm not sure if I could have managed alone.'

'Sure you could,' she said, and she couldn't keep her voice even. 'You've practiced alone for long enough to be really good at it. I know I'm messing with your head, so off you go and practice some more.'

He checked the upper paddock, and every gate. He spent a lot more time up there than he should.

Alex was messing with his head?

Yes, she was. She knew it, too. It was like she could

see right inside him and she knew how terrified he was to think a little boy could need him. And maybe she could sense how desperately he was trying not to care for her.

Don't care, he told himself savagely. *Don't care.*

Caring didn't help. He knew it. The mantra, the feeling of hopelessness, had been drummed into him since he was eight years old. Caring just tore apart both parties instead of one.

Sophie had died and a part of him had died with her. He never wanted to feel like that again.

But Alex was back in the house. Alex with her constant interfering, her prodding conscience, her laugher, her skill, her...

Her status as an employee.

She'd shoved Oliver on to him.

Or not.

Yes, she had. After Brian disappeared he'd caught Oliver up in the top paddock, trying to catch one of the wilder colts.

He'd sent him home with a flea in his ear—the original ogre growling at small children.

It was because Alex was here, Alex with her laughter and her open friendship, that Oliver had dared come back again.

It always came back to Alex.

He walked on. He should go home to sleep.

Sleep? What a laugh.

He walked.

She lay in bed and stared at the ceiling and thought. And thought and thought and thought.

She thought, weirdly, of her family. Of her father who'd pretended to care, had tried to care, but who hadn't pulled it off.

She thought of Jack, trying desperately not to care—and who wasn't succeeding either.

'So throw your hat in the ring,' she whispered into the dark, but she knew he already had, with his offer to teach Oliver, to let him come to the farm whenever he wanted. He couldn't be blind to the unadulterated hero worship in the little boy's eyes. By taking this step, he was exposed, all over again. He was hurting. He'd be hurting right now.

How could she sleep? She lay and stared at the ceiling and thought...and thought.

So many thoughts her head was likely to explode.

Give up.

What was a girl to do at two in the morning if she couldn't sleep?

She could think of nothing but Jack.

Ellie's letter... Surely she had to do something there. What she wanted was to get on a plane and go hug her—but to leave Jack?

No. Next best thing. She switched on her bed lamp and wrote long emails to Matt and to Charlotte. The letter Ellie had sent to Alex had been long and thoughtful and caring, an indication of how close they'd always been, but for some reason this night had her tuned to family nuances. Suddenly she was wondering whether Ellie could have maintained long, thoughtful and caring for two more handwritten letters? When Ellie was delirious about being in love? When relationships in the Patterson family had always been fraught?

So she wrote. Just to check they knew absolutely everything Ellie had told her. Just to tell them she loved them. It helped fill the void where she wanted Jack to be.

The emails were hard. She sent them and they did nothing to make her sleepy.

Family...

Jack.

Do not think of Jack.

Count stars? It had to be better than nothing. The night sky here was breathtaking but the veranda stopped her seeing the stars from her window.

Finally she tugged on the fleecy bathrobe that she'd thought was an indulgence until she'd seen this place. She'd nearly ruined it that first night and it had taken an age to clean but now her bathrobe was her best friend. She padded through the empty house, silent as a mouse, being even more silent past Jack's door.

She slipped out onto the veranda—and Jack was there before her.

He didn't hear her—and for a moment she stayed silent.

The sensible thing would be to retreat. *Now.*

But she wasn't being sensible. There was something about this night. There was something about this man.

A long time ago, sixteen years old, she'd broken her heart over a boy. She'd moped about the house for days and finally her mother had given her a solid talking-to.

'Alexandra, this is your time for having fun,' Fenella had scolded. 'It's time for making friends rather than committing for life. Don't break your heart now. There's no need. One day you'll meet someone so special that there'll be no chance he could ever leave you, or you him.'

'Is that how you feel about Dad?' Alex had whispered, and Fenella had smiled, a weird, tight smile that maybe Ellie's letter had explained. But…

'Of course I do, honey,' Fenella had told her. 'Your dad and I have something special and one day you'll find it, too.'

Had she found it? Here, with this man who was trying so hard not to care? She couldn't know, but what she did know was that she had five months to find out. Starting now?

He was staring out at the moon, staring at nothing, and her heart twisted. Somehow she knew this man. He was strong and silent and wise. He handled his horses with a skill and understanding that took her breath away. He was so good-looking he'd make any woman's heart do back-flips. He was hero material.

And yet it wasn't the hero she was seeing now. She was seeing a boy, desperately caring for his sister, facing a load far too heavy for even an adult to carry alone. She was seeing a man who'd learned that caring hurt.

And today his heart had been tugged right out of the protective shield he'd built for himself, and he was exposed.

In more ways than one.

He'd fallen for Oliver. He'd put the child on a horse— no big deal—but he'd promised to teach him, promised to let him come whenever he wanted. No one seeing Oliver's face could doubt what that promise meant.

It meant every night after school, every weekend, every holiday, Jack would have his personal shadow. Maybe she hadn't seen it as clearly as Jack had, that there were no half-measures in caring.

Up until now he'd held himself back, but today he'd promised to care for Oliver and he'd opened himself to whatever it was that he was most afraid of.

Jack's armour had been shattered.

Tomorrow he might have that armour back in place, she thought. Tomorrow he might have it figured that he could leave an Oliver-size hole but seal the rest.

So tonight...

She'd never had armour where this man was concerned. She'd fallen for him and she was still falling. He was her wonderful Jack, the guy who did things to her insides she couldn't imagine anyone else doing.

And as she watched him in the darkness, she thought this *could* be the man she could love with all her heart. Her mother had promised her she'd meet someone like this, and maybe she had.

So do something.

She sat down beside him on the veranda steps and she took his hand in hers.

'Jack, you were wonderful today,' she said simply. And then she said, 'We have five months together. There are no promises about the future, but for these five months, maybe they could be special for both of us. Maybe it wouldn't hurt if you let me hold you?'

CHAPTER TEN

THE world stilled.

Nothing moved. Nothing breathed. The words hung in the warm night air, waiting to explode.

All or nothing. She was an 'all' sort of girl, she thought ruefully. Her words got her into trouble but she thought it; why not say it?

'Why?' Jack asked at last, in a voice so ragged she wanted to gather him into her arms and hold him for ever.

'Because we both could do with holding?' she managed, trying to make it light but it didn't come out light. Her words came out deadly serious, and she knew she had to say more.

'Maybe...maybe it's more than just holding,' she said, weaving her fingers through his. Feeling the strength of them. 'I'm not sure, but what I'm feeling... I've had boyfriends,' she conceded. 'They've been fun, they've been friends. I thought that was all there was, but now... My mom told me one day wham might happen, and now maybe it has. One look at you and wham.'

'Wham?' he said, sounding astonished, but wonderfully there was a trace of a twinkle returning.

'Well, not completely at first look,' she admitted. 'First you scared me witless, standing in your great black waterproofs in the middle of a rainstorm, spouting all sorts of chauvinistic nonsense. But I saw straight through you. I thought, there and then, Here's a man who I want to hold and I want to hold me right back. This is a man who…'

And then she broke off. She'd been trying to keep it light but it wasn't working.

He was watching her intently, and suddenly there was room for nothing but the truth.

'I don't know,' she said simply. 'I don't know what makes me feel the way I'm feeling about you. How to explain? It's the way you look at me. It's the way you cared for Sancha that first night, and made me a poached egg. It's the way you showed me the platypus, and the way you left me to fix the veranda rail by myself and then didn't go overboard because a mere female had done it. It's the way you trusted me with your horses from the get-go— you respect my training. It's because you make me smile and I know you hurt and I know it almost broke something inside you today when we thought Oliver was dead and I know…I know if these five months are all I can have of you, then I'll take them and gladly. I'll hold you for as long as you want me to hold you.'

Enough. She could lay her heart on her sleeve no further.

She let his hand drop.

She thought about being asked to pack her bags right here, right now. Employee throws herself at her boss…

He was gazing at her in the moonlight, for what seemed like for ever, searching her face as if searching for what he knew was truth.

She met his gaze as calmly as she could, but inside she was anything but calm.

What had she done? Thrown her heart at him, when today he'd been stretched to the limit already? Asked him for yet more commitment?

Asked him to care.

'You feel that…' he said gently, but he didn't move '…about me?'

'Stupid, isn't it,' she said, and suddenly she was choking back a sob. 'I know you don't want it. I know you don't want anyone to care.'

'I didn't think I did,' he said, and finally, finally, he took her hands. He tugged her to her feet and she came, rising so she was hard against him. Her breasts were against the hardness of his chest. 'Alex, I can't….'

'Can't what?' she said, and pressed a little harder. Amazed at her own temerity. Amazed where her body was taking her. 'From where I'm standing if feels as if you definitely can.'

He stilled. Thought about it. Didn't pull away.

'You know, if I didn't care I'd take you to bed in a heartbeat,' he said at last, and she felt his heart beating and thought there was nowhere she wanted to be but right here, right now.

'I thought you didn't care.'

'That was the plan. One crazy vet later…'

'Who's crazy?'

'You,' he said softly into her hair. 'Alex, today, with Oliver… I'm not sure how much you realise how big a deal this is for me. And now, you say you want me.'

'I know,' she whispered. 'It's too much pressure. I should just give you the odd hint. Start by smiling coyly at you over the breakfast table. Maybe carve our linked initials in the stable doors. Send you a valentine—oh, wait, that's done for this year so it's another year away. Sorry, Jack, but I can't wait. You have me now.'

'So what am I supposed to do with you?'

She tugged back at that, looking up at him. Was he looking…trapped?

Trapped?

Whoa. A girl had some pride. Or a girl had to find some pride pretty fast.

She tugged right away and stood and glared at him. 'You needn't worry,' she managed. 'I'm no cavewoman with a club about to drag you off to my lair. I believe I may have said more than was wise. I believe I should retract. Should we go back to calling each other Mr Connor and Dr Patterson?'

She felt humiliated to her socks. She felt sick.

And Jack was still looking at her.

'Alex?'

'What?' It was a huffy sort of reply. Where was her dignity? Back in the States. Maybe that's where she had to go.

'Alex, all I meant to say is that I don't know how this can operate long-term,' he said, and he reached out and took her hands again. 'I made a vow about commitment and I meant it. I said I'd never care for anyone. It causes pain, it doesn't help. I've never seen it work. But yeah, all sorts of things happened today, or maybe they happened a month ago when you first came here but I was too dumb to see it. It seems, like it or not, I do care. Like it or not, I want you.' He took a deep breath. 'I want you in every sense of the word.'

'So…' she said, feeling like she was almost scared to breathe. 'Are you saying you're liking me against your better judgement. Have you read *Pride and Prejudice*?'

'At school but—'

'But you never thought about it again because you think of it as chick fiction,' she said cordially. 'So you didn't learn the Mr Darcy lesson. So here you are, liking me against your better judgement. But you need to think back. Think hard. Mr Darcy got his comeuppance and so might you.'

'I don't understand,' he said, and she believed him. He looked bewildered.

'Neither do dumb males everywhere,' she retorted, and she knew she needed to explain. She must. Because even though a girl had some pride, she wanted this man more than anything else in the world. 'Darcy took almost a whole book to realise he loved Elizabeth, and to know his judgement was just as dumb as his pride. So maybe we could do better. We could put them both aside right there, right now, and just...see. We could just take one woman and one man and put them together and see if we could make each other happy. I'm not saying it'll work. I'm saying we could just...see.'

'For five months.' His face was expressionless.

'That's the contract.'

'Alex...'

'No promises,' she said. 'I know that. But I also know that right now, right at this moment, I want you more than life itself, and I want you to want me right back. And I know for you life is heavy and everything has to be weighed but sometimes I truly believe you should go where your instincts tell you. Heart instead of head. Leap before you look if you like, and consequences be damned. Not that there would be consequences. Except maybe making us very happy for the next five months. So I'm thinking—'

'I'm thinking maybe you might want to stop thinking?'

And amazingly, wonderfully, he was laughing. Laughing!

'Has anyone ever accused you of being able to sell ice to Eskimos?' he demanded.

'Totally different,' she said, twinkling back at him. 'From where I'm standing you haven't seen ice for a very long time.'

He chuckled, a low delicious sound that sent the low simmer in her body into a fiery burn. She wanted…

And so, it seemed, did he. He caught her hands and held, not fiercely, not in the claim of a lover, but in the hold of someone who needed to make sure this was no mere whim.

'Alex, you know I can't make promises.'

'I'm not asking for promises.'

'And yet you're offering to come to my bed.'

'That's a very old-fashioned phrase,' she said. 'And it sounds wanton.' She hesitated. 'You know I'm not wanton.'

'I do know that,' he said gravely. 'And I know the gift you're offering. Alex, a man would need to be a lot stronger than me to resist.'

'I think,' she said softly, almost as a whisper but much more sure, 'that you need to do better than that. I'm not going to bed with a man against his better judgement, no matter how much I want him. I want you to want me. I want you to think we could have a wonderful, wonderful time if we managed to cut loose from our inhibitions for a few months. I'm thinking yes, I could give my heart, and in five months I may well cry all the way home but when I'm in my rocking chair in my nursing home I'll be thinking, Wow, that was mind-blowing, and I'll also be thinking that you'll have a grin on your toothless, ancient face, as well.'

'Toothless?' he said faintly.

'It's sooner than you think. You're really quite old.'

'Hey!'

'I say it as I see it,' she said, twinkling again. 'So I'm saying now, right now, I want you more than anything in the world and if you could just unzip that armour just a little bit…'

'And unzip anything else that came along?'

'That's the one,' she said approvingly. 'If you want me.'

'I do want you,' he said, and the smile died and the grip on her hands tightened. 'Right now, I want you so much it's like there's a black void that I don't know how to fill. Alex, I know nothing about love. I don't do caring. I'm on my own. But you... I just have to look at you and—'

'Your toes curl?' she said hopefully, and he laughed, a lovely, rich chuckle that sounded out over the valley. He tugged her to him and held, long, hard, folding her to his chest, simply holding. Resting his chin on her hair. Folding her to him.

And she didn't say a word. She was fighting with every weapon she had, she thought, but would it be enough? Could this man want her?

'It would be an honour and a privilege to take you to my bed,' he said at last.

'How about fun?' she managed, striving to be light, and he put her away from him, holding her at arm's length.

'Fun, too,' he said. 'But a gift without price for all that. No, I'm not taking you against my better judgement but it is selfish.'

'Two adults who want each other? What's selfish about that?'

'I guess...nothing at all.' He looked down at her gravely in the night. 'Alex Patterson,' he said, soft and low and sure. 'Would you do me the honour of coming to my bed?'

'Oh, for heaven's sake,' she whispered, and then she chuckled. 'I thought you'd never ask.'

He woke and she was spooned into the curve of his body. His face was in her hair. Skin against skin, she was moulded to him, held in his arms.

His.

For he was under no illusions. She'd given herself to him last night, with all the joy and generosity and wonder she possessed. She'd taken him to her as he'd taken her. Their bodies had merged and merged again, and it had felt like...coming home.

There was a peace about him this morning he'd never known, never thought he could know.

Maybe it was this place, he thought. He'd had relationships before—of course he had—but they'd been part of the tight, controlled life he'd built for himself in the city. Here, on this farm that he loved...

Did he love this farm?

There was a thought to let drift with all the others on this magic morning.

He'd loathed this place by the time he'd left it, but it had called him back. The memories of a grandmother who'd truly loved them. The time Sophie was happy. The garden... The horses...

He'd thought his mother's betrayal, Sophie's illness, his grandfather's brutality, had killed it. He'd come here because he'd loved the horses and he'd wanted to be alone, but now...

Now he had a little boy who was depending on him to be his friend and his defender.

Now he had a woman held warm against his body and her heat, her joy, was shattering defences he didn't know he had.

She stirred a little, moving slightly against him, and the feel of her skin on his was enough to take his breath away, to make him forget to think of anything but her, this woman, this warmth, this love.

Love?

He didn't do—

No. He didn't know what he didn't do. For now she was in his arms, twisting to kiss him good-morning, lacing her arms around his neck, kissing him so deeply everything else slid away and there was only this moment, this woman, this joy.

He was hers.

She felt warm and sated and desired.

She felt loved.

For five months?

How could she feel like this about this man, how could she lie with him each night, and walk away after five months?

Don't care, she told herself. Don't think about it. Five months is an eternity. Five months is long enough for miracles to happen.

A miracle had happened. This big, brooding horse whisperer was making love to her with all the tenderness he knew how, with all the love she'd hoped for, with a passion she hadn't known existed.

He was loving her and she was loving him back—and everything else could take care of itself.

Everything else had to take care of itself. All she could think about right now, all she could feel, all she could taste, all she could want, was Jack.

Nothing had changed—yet everything had.

Employer/employee? Not so much. Jack paid her wages. Jack supposedly gave the orders but somewhere during that one night of passion, the dynamics changed.

Equal partners?

This farm needed massive work, but from the moment Alex slipped dreamily from Jack's bed and donned her work clothes, she no longer felt this was a job. She felt like this farm was part of her and she'd do everything in her power to make it wonderful.

Jack valued her as a vet. He'd been reluctant to let her share the heavy work but now she was insisting.

If he was heading down the paddock with the chainsaw, she was there, too. And somehow, this new thing that was between them gave her the power to insist.

'If you chop your leg off, you'll need a vet,' she growled, and he grinned.

'Do you know which way human feet get sewed back on?'

'I have instant surgery techniques on the internet on my phone,' she said with dignity. 'I'll manage.'

So she went with him and his time for being alone was over.

If he'd hated it she would have backed off. That first day as they worked side by side she caught him glancing at her, over and over, as if trying to work up strength to tell her to go. Head back to the house and find her own projects.

But every time she saw that look she'd bounce some-how, make him laugh, make him smile, demand he help her with what she was doing.

He'd relax again—sort of. She knew he wasn't totally relaxed about this new intimacy. She knew he expected it to shatter, but for now they'd work together, and at night they fell into bed again, together. Partners in every sense of the word.

Oliver was giving her joy, too. Jack put him back on Cracker, who was so quiet he'd almost forgotten what it was like to turn on a dime. Not completely, though. Oliver needed to be trained to manage him as a stockhorse, and Alex watched Jack help with wonder.

It was as if he'd shed a skin—or a suit of armour more like. This dark, solitary male was suddenly solitary no longer. She watched him care, she watched him smile and laugh. Occasionally she could see tension. She knew the shadows were there—the armour had been put aside but not thrown away—but she thought, between them, she and Oliver could fight any armour.

In five months?

No. She wasn't going there. Anything could happen in five months. For now, her life was wonderful.

Two weeks later they took delivery of the new windows that made the farm-worker's cottage watertight. Jack could now set it up as a cosy residence. Alex could move in. She could be the independent employee Jack had wanted.

She didn't. Instead, because Alex was in the main house, because the cottage was free, it meant the arrival of Cooper Barratt, an elderly, wiry horseman with hands of magic. This was the man Jack had sought to turn Wararra back into a training stable as well as a stud.

Cooper arrived with his two dogs and his lopsided grin and his lopsided deference. He called Jack 'Jack'—he might be an employee but he deemed himself an equal— but he called Alex 'Missus' and nothing Alex could say would budge him.

'I see the way Jack looks at you,' he said, and grinned. 'If he's the boss, you're the missus. You tell me it ain't true.'

He treated her with more respect than he did Jack and it made her squirm.

'It's me who should be sleeping in the worker's cottage,' she told Jack, and he grinned and hugged her.

'Then we'd have to put Cooper in the big house and the employer/employee relationship would be totally messed up.'

'It's messed up now.' She was lying in his arms, holding him tight, feeling like she had everything she wanted in the world.

'Nothing's messed up,' Jack told her, kissing her hair,

her nose, behind her ear—and then moving on to more intimate places. Places that made her gasp with pleasure.

'For now, things are perfect.'

'For now?' Hard to voice a doubt when he was doing… what he was doing.

'I can't think of tomorrow, my love,' he said huskily into the night. 'I can't think of anything past right now.'

Only he could think.

He woke in the small hours, as he often did, and it was then that the doubts crept in. Alex was curved against his body. She felt wonderful, magic, an extension of himself. She felt perfect.

But perfection didn't last. He cared for her so much, and that in itself was terrifying.

Where were they heading?

Marriage?

There was a thought to take his breath away.

Cooper called her 'Missus.' 'Missus' was the Australian vernacular for the boss's wife. It was a term of respect. It was a term of acknowledgement of what was happening—what had happened.

They were a couple.

If anything happened to her…

His mind closed hard against the thought, and as if she could sense it, she stirred and turned so she was sleepily facing him. Winding her arms around his neck. Kissing him softly.

'Problem?'

See, *that* was the problem. She had him figured. Every time he held back, she sensed it. Every time he worried, she took his worry to her, shared it, forced him to say it out loud.

How could he tell her that the worry was that he cared too much?

How could he take this one last step—abandon fear and step forward with Alex in his arms?

How could he not?

'I'm worrying about resowing the top pasture before the end of autumn,' he managed, and she chuckled and held him closer.

'Liar. You've already ordered the seed. The forecast is for a gentle autumn. You've figured where we can keep the horses until it regenerates.'

'Mmm.'

'You're worried about *we*,' she said softly.

'Alex…'

'Don't,' she said soundly. 'You'll spoil things. For now, for right this moment, we're perfect. For now we have each other in our arms, and we fit like two halves of a whole. I'm not asking or expecting any more of you than that, Jack Connor. For now I'm loving you, and I'm wanting you, but I'm not holding you. My future's in the States, so stop worrying about it.'

'And if I asked that your future could be here?'

She stilled in his arms, but then she looked up at his troubled face and she shook her head.

'You don't want that,' she whispered. 'Not now, at least, and maybe not ever. I'm watching your face and I'm not seeing commitment. I'm seeing something akin to fear. Well, you can quit it with the fear. I come with no strings, Jack Connor, and I'm not letting you attach any. For now, we have now. That's all.'

Afterward he drifted back to sleep again and it was Alex who lay awake and stared into the night.

He'd almost asked her to stay.

· Did she want him to?

Yes. Her head screamed that she was a fool for shushing him, for stopping him asking her to commit. For there was a part of Alex that wanted to commit more than anything in the world.

So what was stopping her taking and holding?

Strangely, it was the thought of her father. Of the letter Ellie had sent her, the letter that lay in the bottom of her suitcase explaining all.

Explaining that her parents' marriage had been built not on the mutual passion she'd always assumed but on reservations, where things weren't quite right, where honesty wasn't first and foremost.

She'd spent a lifetime trying to figure what was wrong with her family. Now she knew, and with that knowledge came the certainty that she didn't want that sort of relationship for herself.

Jack was starting to love her, she thought, but he was loving her despite his reservations. Despite his vows not to care.

As her father had loved her mother despite the fact that she was carrying another man's twins.

Despite...

It was a mean little word, and it stayed with her.

She wanted Jack. She knew that now; there was no *despite* in her language. She'd love him and hold him and care for him and she'd hope, with every ounce of her being.

But she would not let him commit to her *despite...* She wasn't going there. A cold, hard coil of common sense stayed with her.

Her plan had always been to work hard here and then return to the States and find the job of her dreams. Instead she'd found the man of her dreams right where she was.

So yes, if things worked out, if she was sure Jack could

love her, then she'd change her plans in a heartbeat—how could she not?—but she'd watched what *despite* had done to Matt, had done to Ellie.

She would not love this man *despite*.

CHAPTER ELEVEN

WERARRA was blossoming. Autumn crept in, bringing lush pasture, a tinge of cool to the mountain breeze, an added energy to the horses in their care.

With three full-time workers the place was starting to look as it should. Tentatively Jack opened it to buyers. Until now he'd transported sale horses to Albury. Now, with Werarra's reputation growing, with good yards, a showplace that almost matched the website, horsemen from around the country and overseas were welcomed.

He could sell more horses than he could ever supply, Alex thought, but every horse leaving the property was perfect. He insisted on nothing less. So did Cooper, deeply approving of his boss's standards. And so did Alex. She cared for the horses in her charge with passion and she knew when she left this place it wouldn't just be Jack she missed with all her heart.

And so did Oliver.

Every moment he wasn't in school he was here, following Jack wherever he went.

Alex had expected him to adore Cracker, the horse Jack had decreed was his to care for, and he did, but a higher adoration was reserved for Jack.

He was mates with Alex, he respected Cooper and he liked Cooper's dogs. He loved Cracker, but he lived for Jack.

Cooper might be training a recently broken colt. Alex might be treating an older mare with problematic teeth—a procedure that took strength and skill. But if Jack was doing something as mundane as filling up potholes in the driveway, that was the most riveting thing Oliver could dream of to watch, and he did.

'I don't know what to do about it,' Jack said, the night of the pothole filling, and Alex grinned.

'Embrace it? He's doing no harm.'

'It can't last.'

'Why not? You're going nowhere. He'll grow out of hero worship.'

'Yeah,' Jack said roughly, and she knew it still worried him.

He cared, Alex thought. He cared, despite...

There was that word again.

'It's Saturday tomorrow,' she said into the stillness. 'How about we give ourselves a day off?'

'A day off.' He said it like it was another language.

'I've never been up to the far ridge,' she said. 'I was talking to Oliver about it. He says there's a waterfall. His dad took him there once. Do you know it?'

He did. She could see it in his face, but she could also see caution.

'It's five miles,' he said. 'You and me.'

'And Oliver,' she said hurriedly, because there was that *despite* thing again. She and Jack were working side by side, they were sleeping in each other's arms, yet to spend leisure time together seemed another thing entirely. Every night after dinner, Jack disappeared to his study. Alex read or watched television or wrote home. They came together when it was time to sleep, but she knew the thought of further intimacy was yet another step that left him feeling exposed.

She didn't want him exposed. She ached for him to feel that with her he was safe, that with her the terrible loneliness and responsibility he'd faced as a child and young man was over, but she'd do it one step at a time.

A picnic.

With Oliver to diffuse the strangeness of it.

'I know you have more potholes to fill,' she teased gently. 'And I know Oliver's aching to watch you fill them. But all my charges are in fine health, we have no buyers due, Cooper's more than able to hold the fort and I can make sandwiches.'

'Really?' His dark eyes suddenly flashed a twinkle. 'What score sandwiches?'

'Ten if I'd had some notice,' she said, and grinned. 'But because we're picnicking on a whim, they might only be about seven. But my brother tells me my bacon sandwiches are ten even if they look wobbly. What do you say, Jack? Can we take a day and have fun?'

'I should—'

'There are always "shoulds",' she said gently. 'But I really want to see the waterfall. Oliver's offered to take me himself but I don't trust him not to lose us both.'

That was a low blow. Five miles of bushland, they could well get lost and Jack knew it.

'You can't go on your own,' he growled.

'Well, then. Potholes or picnics, what's it to be, Jack Connor?'

And he agreed.

Despite…

Saturday morning. As usual, Oliver arrived before eight and from the moment she broke the news of the impending picnic and saw the glow of undiluted joy on his face, Alex knew it'd be a day to remember.

They rang Brenda to ask permission, but in truth Brenda didn't care. She was accustomed to Oliver spending most of his time on the farm, and Alex thought it was a relief to the woman.

Brenda was doing the 'right thing' by Oliver, but her heart wasn't in it. She'd been saddled with the boy, and she was caring for him *despite*...

Don't think of that word today.

They saddled the horses. They packed the saddlebags with Alex's sandwiches, with fruit, drinks and swimming gear, and they set off.

Cooper came out of the stables to wave them off.

'You look a beaut little family,' he said, and Alex saw Jack's expression change. He had his face under control in an instant, but she'd seen.

A family. He didn't do family.

Would four months be long enough to change something so intrinsic within him?

She refused to worry today.

She'd have a great time today...*despite* misgivings.

There was no way they would have found the waterfall without Jack. Indeed, she would have been lost within ten minutes of leaving the property boundary, she conceded. The bushland here was wild and mountainous. Werarra bordered a national park and there civilisation ended.

The horses nosed their way single file along vague tracks made by wombats or kangaroos. Amazingly they seemed to know where they were going—they needed to because Jack put Alex in front on Rocky, Oliver was in the middle on Cracker, and Jack and Maestro followed at the rear. Keeping watch.

Every now and then, Jack would call a direction, veer

left, slow here, ware low branches, but mostly they rode in silence.

Oliver seemed as awed as she was by the bushland, Alex thought, and knew his father hadn't brought him here often. Indeed, the more she learned of Oliver the more she wondered that his father had done anything for him at all.

He looked a bit small for the horse he was on. His freckled face was intent, his hands gripping the reins tight but not tugging on Cracker's mouth; he was consciously, fiercely, giving his horse his head.

He was a great little kid, Alex thought, and wondered at the deal that had given him a father who walked out on him, and only Brenda, who did her best.

Life wasn't fair. She glanced behind her once again to check him, and Jack was behind him, so she sort of checked on Jack at the same time.

Man and boy—and she knew instinctively that they'd shared harsh backgrounds.

If she was here with Matt right now, he wouldn't be talking either, she thought. Her big brother had been raised with a father who resented him. It had made him turn inward, become a loner.

She had two loners on her hands right now.

The cure?

'I spy,' she said, and got two groans for answer.

'Something beginning with *H*,' she said, doggedly determined, and Oliver gave an oversize, theatrical sigh.

'Horse.'

'Hey, you're a natural,' she said, and grinned. 'Your turn.'

'M,' Oliver ventured.

'Mountain,' Jack ventured, and Oliver beamed like Oliver himself had guessed and won.

'Cool. Your turn.'

'*V,*' Jack said, and Alex turned and met his gaze and he grinned at her and her heart did this crazy sort of back-flip with pike.

Oliver caught the look and stared at Alex, screwed up his nose and yelled, 'Vet!'

Cracker startled, but Jack was right there, grasping his reins, settling him, grinning at the small boy as if this was part of the game.

'Too good, mate. And here's the waterfall.'

Here it was. The creek had been widening as they rode—every time the 'track' neared it, it seemed wider and deeper. Now, one more bend in the track brought them to what the sound of rushing water had been announcing for some time.

It was the most magical place. It had Alex drawing in her reins and drawing in her breath.

'Take that, Manhattan Girl,' Jack said softly, riding up beside her. He must know there was nothing in New York that could possibly compare to this place.

The waterfall wasn't one steep drop, but rather half a dozen tumbles, from rocky plateau to rocky plateau. Vast boulders seemed scattered like marbles, with great mossy banks littered between. A cave beckoned mysteriously behind the water. 'Sophie and I camped in there once,' Jack said, and Alex glanced at him with wonder.

It was the first time she'd heard him talk of his sister with pleasure.

Maybe it was this place, she thought, for how could anyone be unhappy here? Here one could climb or swim or explore the cave or sleep—or simply stay on horseback and look, like she was doing now—but Rocky was already tugging downward to graze on the lush river grasses and Oliver was tumbling from Cracker to explore and Jack was looking at her quizzically as if she really might be comparing the streets of New York to here.

It was perfect.

The beds of moss…

If Oliver wasn't here…

'There is a downside to playing families,' Jack said dryly, and she blushed and he put his hands up and caught her as she slid from Rocky's back—and she knew he was thinking exactly what she was thinking.

'Swim,' he said, his dark eyes twinkling. 'Second best but it'll have to do.'

'It's a pretty poor second,' she retorted, and he hugged her and kissed her and Oliver turned round and saw them and sighed.

'Yuck. Aren't you two swimming?'

'Something beginning with *S*,' Alex managed, hugging Jack right back. Thinking surely this could work. Surely demons could be exorcised to make a happy ever after. 'Three things. Something beginning with *S*, then something with *P* and then something starting with *S*, as well.'

'Swim, picnic and sleep?' Jack demanded, still holding her.

'Sleep?' Oliver demanded, astounded. 'Who'd sleep here? Let's go.'

They swam their hearts out. Oliver adored the cave, declaring it his own secret hiding place, ducking in and out through the falls. Alex organised silly, active duck diving games and had them all playing. They clambered from plateau to plateau of the falls, following the course of the water. They explored every inch of this magic place.

Finally they ate their picnic. Alex curled up on the rug Jack had packed, snuggled Oliver to her—and to Jack's astonishment Oliver did snuggle—and they both closed their eyes.

Alex was sort of leaning against Jack.

Oliver was sort of leaning against Alex.

Family?

'I want to be like this for ever,' Oliver murmured, half asleep. 'Alex can be my mum and Jack will be my dad and I'll have a family.'

And with those few words, Alex felt things change. She could feel tension slam into Jack. The lovely, sensuous, sun-washed sleepiness was gone, just like that.

'Brenda's your mother.' Jack said it mildly but Alex knew it was far from mild. She could feel the stress.

'She doesn't want me,' Oliver said. He still sounded half asleep but he was matter-of-fact about it. He sounded as if he trusted them both, that they were simply an extension of him talking to himself. 'I hear her on the phone. She's got my dad's phone number now and she tells him he has to come and get me. She says, "He's a great kid. You're a louse for leaving us but for dumping him... He's not my kid, Brian, and if you think I'm taking him on so you can swan round playing the bachelor... End of the month or it's social services." And I don't know what social services are.'

The parroting of Brenda's voice was sickening. The whole statement was sickening.

How to respond?

'I guess it means your dad will come and get you by the end of the month,' Alex said, trying to sound sure.

'He doesn't want me,' Oliver said, snuggling further on her knee. She was stroking his hair, and he was soaking her warmth and touch like a puppy might. A lone puppy.

'He hasn't talked to me since he left,' he said, almost matter-of-factly. 'Last time Brenda talked to him she said

"Do you want to talk to him?" and he hung up. But this is so nice.'

And he closed his eyes, like he'd put the conversation away from him as something that no longer affected him—and he went to sleep.

They were left in the sleepy, sun-baked silence. The sound of the waterfall behind them was a gentle wash, a soothing message that all was right with a world that obviously wasn't. The horses were grazing lazily on the lush, grass-coated banks, and the sun-dappled shade gave them the perfect place to sleep themselves.

Alex was still leaning against Jack. She'd been feeling incredibly soporific.

Now all she could feel was his tension.

'I can't,' Jack said as the silence stretched out. As he became sure Oliver was asleep. As they both accepted the unanswered question that hung. He sounding stressed to breaking point. 'I could never—'

'I don't think I could myself,' Alex said cautiously. To take on the parenting of a child such as this one? She was twenty-six years old. She had no idea how to raise a child.

'It takes a village to raise a child,' she whispered. 'I read that somewhere.'

'And he has no one.'

'His dad…'

'I'll hunt the—' Jack stopped himself but she glanced at his face and she thought it was just as well Brian wasn't in range right now. 'I'll hunt him down and make him do what he has to do.'

'How do you force him to love his son?' Alex's fingers were still lightly stroking Oliver's hair. Jack was leaning against the smooth rock face and she was lying against his shoulder. She knew this man so well now, she thought. She'd been sleeping in his arms for almost a month. She knew his body, his smile, his laughter, his depth for loving—and yet she also knew his fear.

He'd failed his sister on his terms. To commit himself to that sort of caring again...

She knew he couldn't. She knew when her six months were up he'd let her go, and she knew he'd let Oliver go now.

Social services? Or the responsibility of Jack caring for another life?

But if Jack couldn't, then who?

The question drifted in her mind, demanding an answer. Who?

Maybe she could. She was starting to love this needful child, this kid who was brave and cheeky—and alone.

Was she crazy? How could she? She wasn't even a resident in this country. To take Oliver back to the US...?

There was surely no way a single American woman could adopt an eleven-year-old Australian. No way in the world.

And Oliver wouldn't want it.

It takes a village. Or two people.

She and Jack?

Jack couldn't commit, even to her.

'If I shift very gently, I can wiggle you back so you're leaning where I'm leaning,' Jack said, already starting to carefully shift. 'I need to go for a walk.'

'Without us?' she asked, and she knew she sounded desolate but there wasn't a thing she could do about it.

'Without you,' he said heavily. 'Alex, some things are just too hard.'

The ride home was made in heavy silence. Alex had hoped that Oliver's request had been a sleepy half dream, a vague, childish notion that he'd forget with the rest of a child's dreams. Instead he rode stolidly home between the two of them, he helped rub down the horses in unaccustomed silence and finally he backed away, preparatory to heading home. No. Heading back to Brenda's. They all knew he didn't think of Brenda's as his home.

'You're not going to, are you?' he asked in a tiny sulky voice that sounded nothing like him. He sounded scared and Alex's heart melted.

And she knew what the question meant. You're not going to care.

'Oliver, I'm going back to America,' she told him, glancing at Jack's grim face and then glancing away fast. 'I'm only here for a while. My family lives in the States.'

'We could be a family.' It was a desperate plea, but his face said he knew before he uttered the words what the answer would be.

'Mate, your dad's your family,' Jack said, and he walked forward and gripped Oliver's thin shoulders. It was meant to be a gesture of reassurance but Alex saw Oliver flinch. Like he knew what was coming. 'Alex has her mum and dad in New York. You have your dad in Brisbane—he's having an extended holiday now but he'll be back. And I have my horses. We don't fit together.'

We could, Alex thought, though the idea was terrifying. Taking on an eleven-year-old... But with Jack?

It takes a village... If she had Jack, she'd consider herself a village.

'It's all right,' Oliver said, but of course it wasn't.

He turned and raced into the dusk.

'Let me drive you home,' Jack called after him, but he was already gone.

That night they lay in each other's arms but things had changed. Things were different.

Things were finished.

It was as if the voicing of Oliver's dream had killed hers. She'd let herself dream.

She lay cradled in Jack's arms; she knew he wanted her, she wanted him with all her heart, but the damage to this man was heart-deep.

He was loving her now against his will.

He stirred a little and she realised he was awake, looking down at her, troubled as she was.

'Alex?'

'You'll let me go,' she whispered.

'I don't know what else to do.'

'You could let me stay,' she whispered back. 'I'd cling like a limpet. I'd care for your horses for ever, mend your verandas.' She took a deep breath. 'I'd love you. I think... I think I already do. The only thing is, you'd have to love me back.'

'I do,' he said softly, but she shook her head.

'Not all of me. Not the me who demands you care for whatever comes with me.'

And he knew what she meant.

The silence stretched on. On and on.

Decision time? Time for the truth. This wasn't just about Oliver. This was about...everything.

'You'd want kids,' he said at last, into the stillness. He was still holding her but there was nothing relaxed about this man. He sounded stretched to breaking. She held him close, skin against skin. She could feel his heart beating against her breast, but it wasn't in rhythm with hers. His heart was pounding.

This was such a big deal....

I should lie, she thought. I could make it just about us. If I can make him love me... Care for me... Commit to me... Then everything else could follow.

But the question was out there, a biggie. To have children...to not have children...

Her father hadn't wanted Matt and Ellie, and what damage had been done by that lack of care?

'Maybe,' she admitted. 'Not right away but yes, maybe I would. And I'd definitely want a dog. Why don't you have a dog, Jack Connor?'

'Dogs need you.'

'Like horses.'

'Not the same way.'

'Yeah, they look at you with great big soulful eyes, something like the way I'm looking at you,' she said.

'Don't look at me like that.'

'I have been for a month,' she whispered, trying hard to keep it light. 'In case you hadn't noticed, I'm smitten.'

'You'd ask me—'

'To care for me,' she said softly, knowing there was only room for truth. 'Yes, I would. And I'd also ask you to care for Oliver and any stray dog I brought home and also any kids we might or might not agree to have. But mostly, Jack, loving you means I want to be loved back. Despite nothing. I'll give you all of my heart, but it's unconditional and if you can't give that back...'

'I can't.' The words were wrenched out of him and she flinched.

'Your sister died,' she said, coldly now because that was the way she was feeling. Exposed and fragile and a little bit angry. Or maybe more than a little bit angry. What was he doing, taking her to his bed every night, loving her with his body, holding her with such tenderness, when it meant nothing? 'Does Sophie's death mean what's between us is dead, too?'

'It never really lived,' he said, and that was where she

drew her line in the sand. Something inside her died a little, right there.

She tugged away, out of his bed. She grabbed the top quilt and wrapped it round her in a gesture of pure defence.

'What was I thinking?' she whispered. He sat up and reached for her but she backed away. 'Don't.'

'Alex.'

'You can't have it both ways,' she managed. 'I didn't seduce you. We fell into each other's arms because we needed each other. Or I thought we needed each other. But if you can't...'

'Maybe I can,' Jack said, sounding desperate. 'If it's just you.'

'There isn't a just me.' Her anger got the better of her then, her history, the letter from Ellie, the sourness that underscored her family. 'That's what my father did. He married my mother—but he only married *her*. There's never been a doubt that he loved her to bits, but she came with strings. She was carrying another man's twins. I'm not carrying twins but I am carrying baggage. I've fallen for a kid called Oliver and if I lived here I'd want to be involved, right up to my neck. I'd want a dog or maybe three. I'd bring home injured wildlife and when and if they died, I'd cry my heart out. And yes, I'd want kids. All those things, Jack, all of them, I'd expect, want, know that you'd share, and you'd share not because you cared for me because that's what my father did and it didn't work, but because your heart was big enough to care for the whole crazy menagerie.'

'Alex...'

'Don't "Alex" me,' she said, backing into the doorway, and she was really yelling now. 'This is what I should have said a month ago. I didn't have it sorted in my head but today...today I wanted to care for Oliver so much, but

I wanted *us* to care. That's what we could be. Jack and Alex. Joined in the caring department. But it's not going to happen.'

'I don't know how.'

'And I don't know how to teach you,' Alex said, flatly now, passion spent and only desolation left. 'My mother couldn't teach my father in all their years of marriage, so what hope do I have? I think…I think we quit this now, Jack. Separate bedrooms. Separate lives. If we can't work together on these terms, then I leave.'

'You can't leave.'

'I should,' she whispered. 'But I don't want to. So…so I'll stay a little longer. But in my bedroom. In my work. If I didn't think Cooper would have kittens, I'd move into the worker's cottage with him, only—'

'There's no need to be ridiculous.'

'There's not, is there,' she said sadly. 'But there is a need to be sensible. That's what we have to be. Starting now.'

She turned and tried for a dignified exit. It didn't happen. She tripped on a corner of the trailing quilt. Jack was out of bed before she fell, catching her, steadying her. Holding her.

She let him hold her for a full minute, savouring the strength, the warmth, her sheer need of this man she'd come to know and love. And then, somehow, she managed to pull away.

She turned and walked down the passage with as much dignity as she could muster.

She hoped he'd call her back.

She hoped he'd follow.

He didn't.

He lay in the dark and missed her. He missed her warmth, the feel of her skin on his, her breath, her tiny movements, the knowledge that he'd let go a woman who could love him.

Who *would* love him, if she was to be believed.

Why wouldn't he believe Alex?

He wanted her. He was hungry for her with a depth he'd never known it was possible to feel.

It was too late to think he couldn't care for her—he knew that he did. When he held her he felt at peace, and the look on her face as she'd backed from the room was well nigh unbearable. That she'd break her heart over him…

She was young, he told himself savagely. Her family was from the other side of the world. She'd go home and she'd get over whatever she was thinking about him.

She'd get over loving him.

So why was that the desirable option? Why did he lie in his bed here and not lunge after her, take her in his arms, love her, promise himself to her, marry her…

It wasn't just Alex.

Loving Alex was commitment enough. To open himself to the vortex of caring, the great, sweet whirlpool that was love, where he cared and cared but could never care enough… Knowing the pain would come eventually, no matter what he did…

That was dumb. The logical part of him knew that what he'd felt for Sophie, what he'd tried to do, what had happened, was nothing to do with how he felt for Alex. But still, loving her, holding her, there was that same sense of standing on a ledge waiting for the world to tilt, so inevitably that falling must happen.

Coward.

He said it to himself out loud and it echoed around the big and empty room with a hollowness that echoed what he was feeling in his heart. You're condemning yourself to…nothing.

You're giving Alex the chance to find happiness with someone who deserves her.

Why was that a good option? He could try to hold her. He'd love her and protect her and care...

And she'd demand that he do the same for Oliver and more. Dogs?

Kids.

Children, dependent on him. Children, when he'd never been able to care for Sophie. He'd looked after her from the time she was six.

Children.

His mind simply blanked at the thought. To bring children into the world, to have someone so utterly dependent...

He thought of Oliver's set face. The pain...

Not Your Problem.

Selfish?

Yeah, maybe he was, but how much better to say at the beginning *I can't*, rather than stand at a graveside and say *I've failed*?

But the look on Alex's face...

No.

The moon outside slipped behind a cloud and the night grew darker. Alex was just down the passage. Distressed. Coming to terms with his cowardice.

She had to do it sometime, he thought grimly. There was no choice.

He should never have loved her.

He had to learn all over again what it was to be alone. He had to let her have a life with someone who cared.

CHAPTER TWELVE

WHAT followed was a week of silence. A week where Alex worked solidly on, intent on her tasks, doing what needed to be doing, seemingly enjoying the horses, seemingly enjoying her increasing friendship with Cooper and the dogs, being pleasant and distant to him.

If he didn't know her well he could almost think there was nothing wrong, but he knew this woman now. He saw the tension lines around her eyes, the flash of pain, quickly disguised, when he appeared. The strain in her voice whenever she spoke to him.

A lesser woman would quit, he thought, but this was Alex. She was here to earn her stripes as a vet on a horse stud, and a little thing like falling in love and being rejected by the owner wasn't about to stand in her way.

Heartbroken? Maybe, but she wasn't showing the world, and she wasn't showing him. She was making it possible for him to get on with his life without her.

Except he still had to watch her. He still had to see her.

He still had to see the way the horses responded to her and feel a searing, aching need deep in his gut.

That had to be put aside.

That was put aside.

Until the day Oliver disappeared.

* * *

The first they knew of it was a phone call just after dark.

They'd worked solidly all day—Alex working with Cooper with the yearlings, Jack working on the outbuildings, making a new roof secure. They were working fast. The weather was oppressively humid, dark clouds thickening through the day. The mother and father of all storms was in the offing and they knew it.

Cooper retired as he always did as soon as the work of the day was done to his solitude in the workman's cottage. Alex cooked but there were no points given any more. She retired to her bedroom but when the phone went in the hall she couldn't help but hear.

Jack's voice was curt and sounded concerned.

'No, he hasn't been here all day. We haven't seen him all week. Brenda, it's dark and with this storm, even if he had been here, I'd have sent him home long before this.'

There was a long silence while Jack listened, and then a terse demand.

'So you haven't seen him since seven this morning?'

She was suddenly out in the passage, pressing against the wall, listening. Watching Jack's face darken with anger. And worry.

'You could have told me... Okay, never mind. Does he have any money? Could he be trying to reach his dad?'

She could hear Brenda now, shrill in defensiveness. And, to give the woman her due, worry.

'Okay.' Jack was raking his hair, looking out through the porch window to the darkness of the storm beyond. 'If Cracker's missing... Does he have mates in town?'

Alex could hear Brenda's silence. It was like a great gaping void.

No mates. No family. Alex's heart seemed to freeze. One little boy and a night when no one should be out.

'I'll be there in ten minutes,' Jack said heavily, and replaced the receiver. He turned and at the look on his face had her reaching out in an automatic need for contact—and then, somehow, she drew back.

'Tell me.'

'Brenda's sister has decided they should buy a house they can share,' he said, his voice bleak as death. 'She's found one, in Brisbane. All of them are moving in. Brenda's sister and her four kids. Brenda and her two girls. But not Oliver. There's not room. Brenda's made an appointment with social welfare in Sydney next Monday. She told Oliver this morning—nicely, she said—that he couldn't keep living with her. She told him she'd find him some nice foster parents—and now he's gone.'

She drove with him—how could she not? The wind was strengthening by the minute, the rain a deluge. Somewhere out there was a child.

Brenda was standing on the veranda, looking distraught. She was staring out into the gathering storm as if she could find him simply by staring.

'It wasn't my fault,' she said before they could say a word. 'I can't keep him. The house has only got two kids' rooms and I can't make my girls share. It wouldn't be right. But we have to find him. The social services said they'll find a foster home.'

'What does he have with him?' Jack said, cutting across her defensiveness. 'We think he's on Cracker. Anything else?'

'I think he took his father's camping gear. I checked. Not the tent, but the sleeping bag. And there's stuff from the grocery cupboard missing. I'll kill him. Of all the stupid—'

'Let's find him first,' Jack snapped. 'Have you called the police?'

'Why would I call the police?'

Because a child's missing, Alex thought. A child, with this storm coming.

Jack stayed silent, his face rigid, staring at Brenda. Then...

'He'll be at the waterfall,' he said slowly. 'That's my guess. If he took camping equipment... He'll be intending to use the cave.'

Alex's heart seemed to still. She thought back to that last day together. Oliver, diving through the waterfall, exploring the cave. Figuring how he could get in without getting wet. Totally fascinated.

The day they were there, though, there'd been little recent rain. Now, the rain was one continuous sheet.

'If he tries to stay in there when the rain comes—' Jack broke off with an oath and headed back into the rain to the car. 'Stay with Brenda,' he growled over his shoulder. 'Tell the police.'

'Brenda can tell the police,' Alex snapped. 'I'm coming with you.'

They collected the horses and rode. There was no other way to get there.

The wind was rising and the horses edged together as though taking comfort from each other. They couldn't ride fast; they were picking their way, making sure each horse had the time to test the ground before setting its weight over a rabbit hole or wombat burrow.

No car could get up here. It was horses or nothing.

Somewhere up here was a child who no one wanted.

Jack was feeling gutted. The horses shouldn't be out in this. Alex shouldn't be out in this. How to make her go back?

He knew her well enough now to know he couldn't.

'I'm taking him back to the States when we find him,' Alex said into the night, and it was like a vow. 'Somehow... There's no way he's being left with foster parents.'

Her statement left him winded. Speechless.

She couldn't mean it.

'Foster parents can be great,' he managed, and she flashed him a look of pure anger.

'But they don't already love him. There's no guarantee they ever will. My family will help me. I can do it.'

'You came out here to get the qualifications to get a job on a ranch as an equine veterinarian. How will having an eleven-year-old child fit in with that?'

'It won't,' she said tightly, trying to control rage. 'But I've fallen in love. It's changed things.'

'With Oliver?'

'Who else do you think I mean?'

'Alex...'

'He'll be fine,' she said, even more tightly. 'If I have to get a job in the city here—get myself a resident's permit—then I will, but if I can get him home it'll be better. The Manhattan apartment's huge. Our maid, Maria, will love him to bits. I can do small-animal work and involve him. He'll like it. Somehow I'll get the right migration permissions. I *can* make it work.'

To say he was gobsmacked was an understatement. She was totally, absolutely serious. She'd change career, change direction, change her life, for a child she'd met less than two months before.

Whereas he...

He was too cowardly to take that first step.

He was afraid of doing harm.

He was afraid of not succeeding.

'That's some generous gesture,' he said at last, and he heard her breath draw in on a hiss.

'Gesture?'

'I only meant—'

'Gesture,' she spat, and Rocky lurched forward, startled. Jack had the reins in an instant.

'Let me go,' Alex said stiffly, collecting herself. 'I'm fine. But this is no gesture. You think I'd play with a child's life? I've thought about it a lot. I've even talked to my brother about it. Matt thinks the migration and custody issues might be prohibitive and while Oliver was safe with Brenda I accepted that, but now...'

'So this isn't an off-the-cuff decision?'

'Amazingly, it isn't,' she managed. 'I can care with my head as well as my heart, Jack Connor. So let's find him and get things moving.' She paused. 'The cave...the water—is it very dangerous?'

'Yes,' he said because there was nothing else to say. The rain had increased sometime during that extraordinary conversation, sheeting down as sleet as well as rain. 'If the river builds... But we can go no faster than we are now.'

'We can if we concentrate,' she muttered. 'We can if we only think of one hoof after another—and nothing else.'

It took them a long time to reach the waterfall, much longer than when they'd set off for the picnic, when there'd been bright sunshine and no rain. But they couldn't push too hard. A lame horse here meant stopping altogether. So Alex rode grimly on, every nerve straining for risk to her horse, for risk to the little boy ahead.

In the past few weeks she'd formed a bond with Oliver that had grown beyond explaining.

Or maybe she could explain it. He reminded her of Matt, her adored big brother. She remembered Matt at Oliver's age, standing before her father, condemned by some minor misdemeanour, stoic. She'd adored her big brother as she'd adored her father and their conflict tore her in two. Matt wrenched at her heartstrings before she even knew such things existed.

And now another little boy, even more needful, was doing the same.

She would help. In that appalling ride her mind settled. She'd already spoken to Matt, sounded him out about helping. He'd been negative—'The thing's crazy, Alex'—but she knew in the end that he'd help.

She could depend on Matt, whereas the man by her side...

She wanted, with all her heart, to depend on Jack.

He'd help tonight. He'd do what he had to do, but he'd go no further. To ask him to commit?

She couldn't. She'd pushed as hard as she could. From here on, she'd cope with this alone.

Something flew at them through the dark and sleet, a disoriented bat, something. Rocky shied and Jack's hands were on her reins, holding, settling.

He was with her, and yet not with her.

Jack...

Oliver. Think of Oliver.

Oliver had to be all that mattered. Jack couldn't love her, but Oliver...she'd love Oliver regardless.

And in the end they found him, quite easily, quite simply. Loneliness, desolation aside, Oliver was one sensible little boy. He'd left the cave when the water started sheeting, but he hadn't thought of going home. Home? Back to Brenda, who didn't want him. He had no options. They found him huddled on the bank of a river that was widening to a roaring torrent, soaked to the skin, holding Cracker's reins and simply waiting for what happened next.

Or expecting that nothing would.

The lightning was now almost one continuous sheet. They could see Oliver's silhouette against the riverbank. They could see his heaving shoulders, but as they approached there wasn't a sound. Even in despair, Oliver's sobs were silent.

Jack saw him, and Alex spotted him almost in the same instant. She was off her horse. Rocky's reins were thrust into Jack's hands and Alex was crouched beside him, tugging him to her, enfolding him to her in the age-old way a woman comforted a child she loved.

Loved.

Who could doubt it, the way she held him. Jack knew, looking at them both, that this was surely what he was seeing.

He had to see to the horses. When Alex reached him, Oliver had released Cracker's reins. All the horses were edgy with the thunder and lightning. He gathered them together, led them under the slight shelter of the cliff face so they were away from the frightening rush of water—thankfully at the foot of this waterfall there was little risk of lightning strike—and then he returned.

They were still entwined. Woman and child.

She cared with all her heart.

And so did he. He watched and things were twisting inside.

Or maybe not twisting. Maybe they were unravelling. A dark and bitter knot was being untied, let free.

His mother's words came back to him…

Take care of your sister.

He'd been eight years old.

It was like clearing mists. As he watched Oliver cling to Alex as if he'd been drowning, he thought, *I was three years younger than Oliver is now.*

And then he thought, *How can a child do anything but fail when given such a task?*

And the bitter sense of failure turned to something else. Something it should have been all along.

It turned to anger at a mother who could have made such a demand. It turned to anger at a grandfather who took it as read that Sophie was Jack's responsibility.

How could you have asked the impossible of me?

'I was eight years old,' he said to himself, and then he looked at what was before him and he said what had to be said.

'I couldn't do it then, but I can do it now.'

And then he walked across to the riverbank, to the crouched figures huddled in the driving rain. He hauled off his great sou'wester and he covered them all. And then, because his makeshift tent was tiny, because they had to be close and because he wanted to be close more than anything else in the world, he tugged them to him.

Both of them.

And they turned and melted into him, just like that. He held them against him. He felt their hearts beating against him. He felt Oliver's sobs subside and he felt Alex's breath against his face.

He felt her hold him as he was holding her, with Oliver sandwiched between them, and he felt a promise being made. The promise felt good. It felt right.

No matter the storm, here was home.

Here was caring.

Here was love.

Jack put Oliver before him, on Maestro, while Alex led Cracker. They didn't take him back to Brenda. They took him to Werarra. *Home.*

The little boy was past speech, past questions, past anything but clinging to Jack as he carried him into the house.

He was eleven years old but tonight he seemed so much younger.

The Wombat Siding cop was there, with Cooper. They'd been about to organise a wider search.

Jack watched Cooper's face break into a vast grin as he saw Oliver. He watched Cooper's dogs make a fuss of the little boy and he thought, Cooper was another he'd end up caring for.

For Cooper was already doing his share of caring.

And finally, finally, he was starting to get it. The load he'd been given as a child had been too great, but the concept was wonderful. You cared, and you were cared for right back.

Cooper disappeared to see to the horses, looking a bit embarrassed at the emotion. The cop left, relieved, and Jack thought there was another example of caring. Country cops... It was what they did.

Jack phoned Brenda, and heard her relief that Oliver was found, and heard even more relief that he'd like him to stay at Werarra for the night.

He had to stay at Werarra, for Jack knew a decision had been made.

Alex had Oliver in a hot bath before the phone call was ended. She washed him and teased him and made him smile a little, then towelled him dry, while Jack found a huge T-shirt for him to wear to bed.

In the end she even had the bedraggled little boy giggling at the sight of himself in the mirror. It wasn't a very loud giggle, but it sounded fine to Jack.

'He can sleep in my bed,' Alex said, and Jack shook his head.

'Let's put him in ours. Oliver, can you cope with sleeping between the pair of us?'

And Alex met his gaze over Oliver's head and something happened to her face.

Something wonderful.

So they tucked him into Jack's big bed and Jack sat on the end of the bed and watched as Alex cradled him and told him people loved him and nothing bad would happen and she thought she might buy him a puppy.

A puppy.

She'd take that on, too, he thought.

Nothing had been said. Nothing had been promised between them. What she was saying to Oliver now stood as a sole promise.

She'd keep that promise, he thought. She'd take a small boy back to Manhattan. She'd face down immigration and social services. She'd cope with quarantine and caring for a child and his puppy in New York. Alone.

It wasn't going to happen. Not if caring could help it.

Finally Oliver slept. Finally he could say what needed to be said.

But there were practicalities. They'd ridden together in the storm, and they looked and felt like it.

'Now it's our turn for a bath,' Jack decreed, and Alex looked at him and smiled, almost shyly.

'Together?'

'How can you doubt it,' he said, and smiled at her and held her and then washed every lovely inch of her. As she did him.

Finally they dried each other, and then they held each other for a long time after. They simply held. This night was too wonderful, too fragile, too precious, to take it any further.

Finally they slipped into bed, one on either side of a deeply sleeping child.

'We'll have to restore another bedroom, really fast,' Jack said softly into the night. 'He's going to be insecure for quite a while. What if we put a door through to next door—we can leave it open if he has nightmares. Then, when he gets older and feels more at home, we can give him the attic room. A teenager with his dog would like that. Maybe then…maybe then our adjoining room could be used for babies.' He hesitated again. 'That is, if you'd like babies.'

He heard her intake of breath. He heard a silence that went on and on. He couldn't reach for her—there was a child between them—but maybe that was just as well. He'd been less than perfect in his approach to this woman. Maybe she needed time to think.

'You'd take that leap of faith?' she whispered.

She knew. She understood. And he thought, She's always understood.

What makes a woman love a man? What makes a woman understand a man almost before he understands himself?

'I love you, Alex,' he said softly into the dark. 'I think I loved you from the moment I saw you, angry and wet and righteous. And now I love you more. You're brave and funny and clever, and you've beaten me seventeen times to my nine in the cooking stakes. And you lie here in my bed.'

'With a child between us…'

'See, that's what I've finally figured,' he said, figuring it still as he spoke. 'No matter the shadows, no matter what physically separates us, there's nothing between us. I'm not a man of pretty words, Alex. Maybe I never will be, but I'll try. Because I'm tired of being alone. Being alone was a survival technique before I knew you existed in the world, but my survival's changed. It's changed with loving you. Now my survival depends on one great-hearted vet. On one slip of a girl. It depends on you loving me. It depends on you letting me care, and on me caring right back.'

'Oh, Jack...' She sounded like she was almost afraid to speak. She sounded awed. 'But...babies even?'

'Caring comes in all forms,' he said, surely now, knowing this was right. 'I've figured it. If you're going to care, you might as well let in the whole human catastrophe. You, my love. Oliver. That puppy you just promised him. Cooper, maybe—he's a curmudgeonly old bachelor, but we both saw today how much he cares already and how can we not care back? His dogs. Our horses. All of this I'll care for—but mostly I care for you.'

She didn't answer. It seemed she couldn't.

He lay back in the dark and thought of all the ways a man should say what he wanted to say. After a romantic candlelight dinner? In a hot-air balloon? Via luxury cruises, roses, hearts and flowers?

But this was here, this was right, and this was real.

'Alexander Patterson,' he said simply into the dark. 'Would you do me the honour of becoming my wife?'

And from the darkness, from the other side of the sleeping child, came the answer he seemed to have been waiting all his life to hear.

'Why, yes, Conner,' she said simply. 'Yes, my love, I believe I will.'

* * * * *

Mills & Boon® Hardback

October 2012

ROMANCE

Banished to the Harem	Carol Marinelli
Not Just the Greek's Wife	Lucy Monroe
A Delicious Deception	Elizabeth Power
Painted the Other Woman	Julia James
A Game of Vows	Maisey Yates
A Devil in Disguise	Caitlin Crews
Revelations of the Night Before	Lynn Raye Harris
Defying her Desert Duty	Annie West
The Wedding Must Go On	Robyn Grady
The Devil and the Deep	Amy Andrews
Taming the Brooding Cattleman	Marion Lennox
The Rancher's Unexpected Family	Myrna Mackenzie
Single Dad's Holiday Wedding	Patricia Thayer
Nanny for the Millionaire's Twins	Susan Meier
Truth-Or-Date.com	Nina Harrington
Wedding Date with Mr Wrong	Nicola Marsh
The Family Who Made Him Whole	Jennifer Taylor
The Doctor Meets Her Match	Annie Claydon

MEDICAL

A Socialite's Christmas Wish	Lucy Clark
Redeeming Dr Riccardi	Leah Martyn
The Doctor's Lost-and-Found Heart	Dianne Drake
The Man Who Wouldn't Marry	Tina Beckett

Mills & Boon® Large Print

October 2012

ROMANCE

A Secret Disgrace	Penny Jordan
The Dark Side of Desire	Julia James
The Forbidden Ferrara	Sarah Morgan
The Truth Behind his Touch	Cathy Williams
Plain Jane in the Spotlight	Lucy Gordon
Battle for the Soldier's Heart	Cara Colter
The Navy SEAL's Bride	Soraya Lane
My Greek Island Fling	Nina Harrington
Enemies at the Altar	Melanie Milburne
In the Italian's Sights	Helen Brooks
In Defiance of Duty	Caitlin Crews

HISTORICAL

The Duchess Hunt	Elizabeth Beacon
Marriage of Mercy	Carla Kelly
Unbuttoning Miss Hardwick	Deb Marlowe
Chained to the Barbarian	Carol Townend
My Fair Concubine	Jeannie Lin

MEDICAL

Georgie's Big Greek Wedding?	Emily Forbes
The Nurse's Not-So-Secret Scandal	Wendy S. Marcus
Dr Right All Along	Joanna Neil
Summer With A French Surgeon	Margaret Barker
Sydney Harbour Hospital: Tom's Redemption	Fiona Lowe
Doctor on Her Doorstep	Annie Claydon

Mills & Boon® Hardback

November 2012

ROMANCE

A Night of No Return	Sarah Morgan
A Tempestuous Temptation	Cathy Williams
Back in the Headlines	Sharon Kendrick
A Taste of the Untamed	Susan Stephens
Exquisite Revenge	Abby Green
Beneath the Veil of Paradise	Kate Hewitt
Surrendering All But Her Heart	Melanie Milburne
Innocent of His Claim	Janette Kenny
The Price of Fame	Anne Oliver
One Night, So Pregnant!	Heidi Rice
The Count's Christmas Baby	Rebecca Winters
His Larkville Cinderella	Melissa McClone
The Nanny Who Saved Christmas	Michelle Douglas
Snowed in at the Ranch	Cara Colter
Hitched!	Jessica Hart
Once A Rebel...	Nikki Logan
A Doctor, A Fling & A Wedding Ring	Fiona McArthur
Her Christmas Eve Diamond	Scarlet Wilson

MEDICAL

Maybe This Christmas...?	Alison Roberts
Dr Chandler's Sleeping Beauty	Melanie Milburne
Newborn Baby For Christmas	Fiona Lowe
The War Hero's Locked-Away Heart	Louisa George

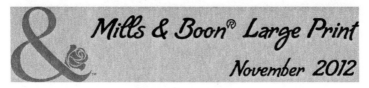

ROMANCE

The Secrets She Carried	Lynne Graham
To Love, Honour and Betray	Jennie Lucas
Heart of a Desert Warrior	Lucy Monroe
Unnoticed and Untouched	Lynn Raye Harris
Argentinian in the Outback	Margaret Way
The Sheikh's Jewel	Melissa James
The Rebel Rancher	Donna Alward
Always the Best Man	Fiona Harper
A Royal World Apart	Maisey Yates
Distracted by her Virtue	Maggie Cox
The Count's Prize	Christina Hollis

HISTORICAL

An Escapade and an Engagement	Annie Burrows
The Laird's Forbidden Lady	Ann Lethbridge
His Makeshift Wife	Anne Ashley
The Captain and the Wallflower	Lyn Stone
Tempted by the Highland Warrior	Michelle Willingham

MEDICAL

Sydney Harbour Hospital: Lexi's Secret	Melanie Milburne
West Wing to Maternity Wing!	Scarlet Wilson
Diamond Ring for the Ice Queen	Lucy Clark
No.1 Dad in Texas	Dianne Drake
The Dangers of Dating Your Boss	Sue MacKay
The Doctor, His Daughter and Me	Leonie Knight

WEB/M&B/RTL3 HB

Discover Pure Reading Pleasure with

**Visit the Mills & Boon website for all
the latest in romance**

Buy all the latest releases, backlist and eBooks

Find out more about our authors and their books

Join our community and chat to authors and other readers

Free online reads from your favourite authors

Win with our fantastic online competitions

Sign up for our free monthly eNewsletter

Tell us what you think by signing up to our reader panel

Rate and review books with our star system

www.millsandboon.co.uk

 Follow us at twitter.com/millsandboonuk

 Become a fan at facebook.com/romancehq